Outback Escape:
The Sister

ANNIE SEATON

The Augathella Girls: Book 3

ANNIE SEATON

ISBN 978-0-6454843-6-6

Dedication

For the residents of Morweh Shire who gave me such a fabulous welcome!

ANNIE SEATON

The Augathella Girls series.

Book 1: Outback Roads –The Nanny

Book 2: Outback Sky – The Pilot

Book 3: Outback Escape – The Sister

Book 4: Outback Winds – The Jillaroo

Book 5: Outback Dawn – The Visitor

Book 6: Outback Moonlight – The Rogue

Book 7: Outback Dust – The Drifter

Book 8: Outback Hope – The Farmer

Augathella Characters-Book 3

Sophie Cartwright	*Kilcoy Station*
Kent Mason	*Lara Waters*
Kimberley Riordan	Sophie's friend
Callie Young	Braden's partner
Fallon Malone	Helicopter pilot
Rory, Nigel and Petie	Sophie's nephews
Braden Cartwright	Sophie's brother
Jon Ingram	Station Manager
Amelia Foley	Jillaroo
Ben Riley	Shire Council Inspector
Jennifer Shaw	School Counsellor
Jim Anderson	Local garage owner

Chapter 1

Sophie

In the month since her brother, Braden, and her ex, Kent Mason, had brought her home from the cattle station at Innot Springs, Sophie Cartwright had picked up four to five shifts each week at the bistro in the local pub at Augathella. Much to Braden's disapproval, she'd also couch-surfed at several of her friends' places, ignoring his pleas for her to come home to *Kilcoy Station.*

As she wiped down the last table in the dining room, ready to knock off and head back to her friend Kim's house, Sean—the chef with wandering hands—poked his head into the dining room.

'Sophie, there's a bloke at the back door wanting to see you.'

Sophie stood stock still, her heart thumping hard. 'Who is it?'

'I dunno. I didn't ask. A big bruiser.' Sean came into the dining room and she took a quick step back. 'You okay? You look washed out all of a sudden.'

'He didn't say his name?'

Surely Jock wouldn't have the hide to come here looking for her?

'Nuh. Listen I'll hang around while you talk to him.' His grin was crafty. 'And then we can have a staffie drink when you're finished.'

'Thanks, but no. I have somewhere to go. I'm fine. I'll just stick my head outside and see who it is.'

Sean shrugged and went back to the kitchen while Sophie slipped the white waitressing apron over her head. Scrunching it up, she placed it in the linen bag with the tablecloths and napkins waiting for the laundry collection that came through from Charleville twice a week. Making her way over to the back of the bistro, she stood to the side of the open window, but it was too dark to see who was waiting out there for her. All she could see was the glowing tip of a cigarette.

Her heart thumped hard and she tried to breathe easily. Walking into the kitchen, she nodded at Sean. 'If you could just wait here for a sec, I'll see who it is.'

'It'll cost you a drink.'

'All right. One drink, then I have to go.' Sophie gave in; one drink wasn't a commitment. Sean was new in town, and he wasn't a bad guy. A bit touchy-feely but she'd coped. She knew his type; he'd stay here for a few weeks and then move on to the next small town. Maybe when he did, she could talk to the publican and offer to take over the cooking. She'd do a better job than Sean.

Sophie went to smooth her hair back and then stopped. If it was Jock outside—the man she'd shared a house with for two years and recently fled from—she'd be inside in a flash. The only others it might be would be Braden or Kent, but neither of them smoked.

'Are you gonna go out there or are you going to stand there biting your lip all night?' Sean flicked off the lights in the kitchen.

'All right, I'm going.' Sophie took a deep breath and slowly pushed open the screen door. It creaked as the figure of a man stepped towards her, a cigarette hanging in his hand.

'Sophie, you're late knocking off?'

She put her hand to her chest. 'Braden! What are you doing skulking around the back, and more to the point, what are you doing smoking? I thought you gave up years ago!'

'I did.'

'Hang on a minute.' Sophie called back into the kitchen 'It's okay, Sean. It's my brother. I'll see you Saturday night.'

'And don't forget, you owe me a drink,' Sean yelled back.

Sophie turned to her brother. 'Do we have to stand out here near the garbage bins? Come into the front bar.'

'No. I want to talk to you.'

'We can talk there.'

'No. I want to talk to you privately.' His voice was tense. 'That's why I'm smoking. It calms me. I have some things I want to say to you.'

'Maybe I don't want to hear them.'

'You probably don't, but it's time you listened to me. Come on, we'll walk up to the park. We can sit there.'

'Where's Callie?'

'She's home with the boys. I had to come to town for a meeting tonight so I figured I'd wait and see you. I didn't think you'd be so late finishing work.'

'There are a lot of tourists in town. Ready for Easter.'

'Where are you staying now?' her brother asked.

'At Kimberley's place.'

'I need you to come home, Soph.' He shook his head and dropped the cigarette butt and grinding it out with the heel of his boot. 'No, I *want* you to come home. There's a difference.'

'We can stay here and talk. It won't take long.'

'You reckon? You mightn't like it. I'm not going anywhere until I deliver some home truths.'

'So I'm not going to like it, hey?' Sophie folded her arms. 'And why should I listen to you?'

'Because it's about time you did.'

'Say whatever you have to, and then I need to go. Kim's waiting for me.' Her words were clipped. She knew exactly what Braden wanted to find out, but she had vowed to herself that Jock was in the past and she wasn't going to think or talk about it.

'Right.'

To Sophie's surprise, Braden's hand shook as he lit another cigarette.

'You're twenty-five years old, and it's time you took some responsibility,' he said.

Sophie's temper began a slow burn but she didn't speak and his next words shocked her.

'You broke off with Kent. A damn good man that you should be married to by now. You broke his bloody heart, and then you took off with that no-hoper. And then you moved away with him to that hovel we rescued you from. And now you're freeloading at any place in Augathella that'll put you up. What the hell is going on in your head, Sophie?'

Sophie took a step forward and poked her brother in the chest. Hard.

'Ouch.'

11

'Put that damn cigarette out and listen to me. As much as you're peeing me off, I don't want to see you die of lung cancer. For your boys' sakes. *I* don't care what you do.'

'You do, you know.'

'Okay, I do, but you have no right to speak to me like that. I didn't break up with Kent. *He* broke up with *me*.'

'That's not what he said.'

'So I'm a liar now too, am I?'

'No.' Braden ran a hand through his hair.

'Well, you ask Mr Perfect Mason what he did and why I broke it off. I'm not always in the wrong, Braden, although everyone seems to believe that. Mum and Dad always did, and now you're doing the same.'

'I want you to come home, Sophie. I'm worried about you, and you still haven't told me why you were so bloody scared of Jock. I'm not stupid. I saw the bruises on your wrists. You seem—I don't know—you seem lost.'

Sophie blinked tears away. 'All right. I am lost, and why shouldn't I be? Who has ever cared about me in this godforsaken place?' She focused on keeping her voice level and not crying. 'And how *dare* you tell me I have no responsibility? Who looked after your three little boys when Julia died? When you couldn't cope with them?'

Braden flinched. 'You did and I appreciate that more than you'll ever know.'

'So leave me alone now. Let me sort it out myself. I need to escape this town. I need to start somewhere new.'

'Doing what? And where?'

'I have some options.'

'No, I want you to come home.'

'Maybe for a short while. I'll think about it.'

'I'm not leaving until you agree.'

'All right. I'll come home if I can move into the donga.'

'They're both taken.' Braden shook his head. 'We've got new staff going in there. I'm building a new one too.'

This time Sophie knew she had the upper hand. Braden would never agree to what she was going to suggest, although it was way past time that he did.

'I'll move into the side of the house you closed down. Have you cleaned out Julia's stuff yet?' she asked bluntly.

'No.' His mouth set in a straight line.

'It's about time you did. It's not fair to Callie to have all Julia's stuff in that half of the house. I'll come home and help you clean it out and I'll move in there. It's not right that I live in that side of the house with you and Callie and the boys. What do you have to say to that?'

Braden looked at her for a long moment, and then he nodded. 'You're right. It's past time. I'll think about it.'

Sophie was lost for words for a minute. She hadn't expected Braden to agree so readily. She put her hand on his arm. 'It will be a step forward, Bray. And if you're as serious about Callie as I think you are, you need to do it. We'll always remember Julia, and I'll help you tell the boys about her as they grow.'

'That'll be a bit hard if you don't live here,' he said gruffly, but she knew it was now more emotion than temper that filled his voice.

'Wherever I end up, I hope they'll visit me.'

'Of course, they will.'

Chapter 2

Sophie

'Kim, have you got some spare shampoo, even one of those little motel ones? I forgot to bring mine.' Sophie poked her head around the bathroom door of Kimberley Riordan's house with a towel wrapped around her body.

'Sure, in the third drawer in the vanity and don't laugh. I'm a serial shampoo collector. Good to see one being used. Don't be long though. The bus comes at six.' Kim's laugh brought a smile to Sophie's face, something that had been a rare occurrence since Braden—and Kent—had flown north to bring her home. During the flight back from the north, she'd been so relieved to be going home, she'd managed to ignore the angst between her and Kent. Or more like the angst from Kent.

Talking to Braden last night had made her think about Kent way too much. Kent had barely spoken to her since she'd come home. So, they'd been an item when they were younger, move on, it was time he got over it. She had.

Liar, liar pants on fire, her conscience nagged at her.

15

'I have,' Sophie muttered crossly to herself as she rummaged through the array of shampoo in the drawer. Kim was right; there was a selection and a half, and the drawer was full. She took a tube each of shampoo and conditioner and turned the shower on.

She had more on her mind than worrying about Kent Mason. Besides, by the look of things he'd taken up with that new part-time teacher at the school. She'd seen them together twice this week.

Sophie had to decide what she was going to do about going home to *Kilcoy Station*. And she had to decide what to do tomorrow. She'd couch-surfed around half a dozen friends' places since she'd come back to the district. Kim's sisters were coming home to Augathella for Easter, so Sophie was moving on. It was a big weekend in town with the mystery fundraiser tonight, the billy cart races and rodeo on the weekend, and then the races on Monday.

Sophie pulled a face; she had no choice. She'd have to go back to the station. Braden had taken her stuff there when they'd flown home from up north, plus she'd need to get one of her good dresses and a fascinator if she was going to go to the races on Monday. Maybe she wouldn't go. Sometimes Sophie wondered if she was suffering from depression. Since she'd come home she found it hard to get enthusiastic about anything. She didn't want to be in Augathella, but she sure didn't want to be at Innot Springs with Jock. She didn't know where she wanted to be; this restlessness was not her usual mood.

Braden was sorted and Sophie was sure he didn't need her out at *Kilcoy Station*, no matter what he'd said last night.

Before he'd left to go home last night, he'd almost begged her.

'Soph, please come home. I need you. With Callie at school for three days a week, and the new jillaroo not here yet, things are hectic.'

'I thought you were going to hire a cook and a housekeeper? If I do come home, is that what you're after?'

'If you want to do that, I'll put you on the books.'

'Don't be stupid. You're not going to pay me.'

'It's not stupid. It's work. If you come, I'll pay you.'

'I've got a job at the pub.'

'Please, Soph.'

'I'll think about it.'

Sophie worried that it would be too awkward. Braden and Callie were in a new relationship, and now Callie had moved into the house. As a new couple they were good together and Sophie really liked her brother's new partner. Braden was happy and the boys had settled, especially poor little Nigel. She'd seen the boys in town a couple of times and they'd been ecstatic to see her.

If the dongas had been empty Sophie would have gone back home like a shot, but apparently, a new jillaroo was starting work at *Kilcoy Station* next week, and the other donga was being used by one of the contract station hands for a few months.

Braden, Callie, and the kids would be at the fundraiser tonight, so maybe she'd sit down with Callie and have a chat, see what she thought about it.

Maybe.

Going home would be the smartest thing to do, but there were the boys to consider too. She'd looked after Rory, Nigel, and Petie for so long, that they'd become reliant on her and she didn't want to put a spoke in Callie's wheel, so to speak.

'Hurry up, Soph,' Kim called. 'We've got fifteen minutes before the bus gets here. What are you wearing? I can't decide.'

'Jeans and a jumper.'

'Get a bit glammed up, though. It's going to be a big night.'

Sophie quickly dried off, wrapped her hair in a towel and headed for the spare bedroom to dig out her clothes. Two minutes to get dressed, two minutes to slap on some makeup, five minutes to dry her hair, and she knew she'd be ready before Kim was. Digging in her suitcase, she searched for the scoop-necked black bodysuit. She could wear it with her washed-out denim jeans and a vest; it would get cool out there tonight.

Her hair dried quickly and she scooped it up into a ponytail, grabbed her sparkly vest, put her boots on and hurried down the hall.

'You ready yet, Kimbo?'

'Almost. Be a love and grab my green ankle boots from the laundry. I'll meet you out the front. The bus is picking us up at the gate.'

Sophie did as she was asked and waited out on the front porch. Kimberley lived in her grandparent's house overlooking the river. The soft afternoon light filtered through the trees on the river bank and the breeze lifted the lacy fronds of the Moreton Bay Ash that stood sentinel near the bridge.

'Kim, three minutes,' she called.

Footsteps hurried up the hall, and Kim raced out, pulling the door shut behind her. She grabbed her boots and slipped them on over her socks. 'Thanks, you're a love. How is it that I can organise a class of twenty-five children with no problem, but can never be on time for any of my stuff!'

'You've always been the same,' Sophie teased. 'I remember when you used to go out in Braden's group, they always left you until last to be picked up.' She picked up the bag where she'd put a jumper and a bottle of water. 'Now tell me about this mystery outing. Why the secrecy?'

'I wanted it to be a surprise, but I guess we'll be there soon. It's a fundraiser for the school, and Craig has offered his property. You know that big camp kitchen area at his place where the grey nomies camp? Near the hot bore?'

'I love that bore. Has he still got the bathtubs alongside it?'

'Yeah, he's booked out for weeks ahead, now that the weather's cooling down. He said it was a good idea to have the function at his place because he'd have a captive clientele to spend money. Jim Anderson has let us have the three school buses to take everyone out there, and pick up at stations along the way.'

'Sounds super organised.' Sophie nudged Kim. 'Did Bob Hamblin organise it?'

'No, Jacinta Mason did.'

Kent's sister. That would mean he'd be there. One thing she'd always admire about Kent's family was their closeness and their ready affection. It had been so different to her and Braden's experience growing up. Their parents had been old school, with not a lot of overt affection displayed, but expectations clearly defined. Kent's parents had welcomed her to their station when she and Kent had started seeing each other in Year 12 after Sophie had begged to be allowed to leave boarding school and do her final year at the local high school.

'I suppose you've learned all you need by now, Dad had said. 'No need for university for you. You can help your mother around the station.'

Their father had old-fashioned values and old-fashioned views, and Sophie had seen a different world at *Lara Waters* when she and Kent had become an item. A world where her needs and hopes and dreams were respected. Kent's parents, Rhonda and Garth, had welcomed her with open arms, and as Sophie spent more time out there, she realised what a different household she and Braden had been brought up in. All that mattered at their home was the work ethic. Unfortunately that hard work had shortened the lives of both their parents.

There had been few family occasions and little time for celebrating life. Christmas had been celebrated with one gift each—a useful gift—and a baked dinner, and then back to work. Easter was a non-event, and when Kent gave Sophie an Easter egg the first year they had been together, he had been shocked to discover it was the first one she'd ever received.

They'd been lying on the grass out near the hot bore at the back of *Lara Waters*, watching the clouds above.

'So for real? No Easter bunny ever?' he said.

'Nope.'

'Santa Claus?'

'No, just a present from Mum and Dad. Always something we could use. The Christmas before my first year at boarding school I was given a pen and pencil set.'

Kent had rolled over and kissed her and there had been a lull in their conversation for quite a while.

'What about the tooth fairy?' he'd asked later that afternoon when they were soaking in the warm bore water.

'Nope. Hadn't heard of it until I was in late primary school. I had all my second teeth by then.'

She and Kent had split the week before the accident, but she pushed away the thoughts of that time. Jock had stepped in and cheered her up, and before she knew it, he'd asked her to move in with him. To his credit, he had been supportive when Julia had died, and he'd agreed to have the boys stay with them until Braden sorted himself out.

When she was looking after the boys after Julia's death, Sophie had ensured their lives were full of those special occasions; Santa Claus, the

Easter Bunny, and the Tooth Fairy had been regular visitors in their household, much to Jock's disgust.

Sophie let out a regretful sigh now as she sat beside Kim.

'You okay?' Kim asked. 'Why the big sigh?'

'Yep. I was just thinking about Jacinta and Kent's parents. They're lovely people.'

'They are. Rhonda is an absolute hoot. You can always hear laughter when she comes to do the volunteer reading at the school. We miss her. Do you know how long they're away for?'

'No. I've just heard they've gone on a trip.'

'Yep, a cruise, Jacinta said.' Kim looked at her curiously. 'Doesn't Kent keep you up to speed? Do you see much of him these days?'

'No, but he was at the pub having dinner with the new school counsellor the other night.' No one else knew the acrimonious circumstances of their break-up. Not even Braden. If he'd known what Kent had done, he wouldn't have asked him to fly up to Innot Springs to bring her home. Kent should have said no.

'Oh, God, I'll have to warn him. Jennifer's latched on to every single man in town. The male teachers at school almost run when they see her coming. She's an absolute pain. From all accounts, she wants to find a husband and settle out here.'

'Kent's a big boy now.' Sophie was hoping he'd be busy and not at the fundraiser tonight. It was much easier not to spend time in his company. No matter what had happened, and what he'd done to her, he still made her heart race. Well, she'd be able to get lost in the crowd if there were that many coming from town and the surrounding district.

'Are you okay with Kent these days? You never told me why you broke up.'

'That was a long time ago.'

'But you were so good together, Soph. We all thought there'd be a wedding.'

And so did I, Sophie thought.

Kim looked at her, waiting for her to spill. 'Why did you break up?'

'Kent let me down.' Sophie was relieved to see the school bus come around the corner. 'Here's the bus,' she said.

'I bags the back seat if it's free.'

Sophie chuckled and shook her head, pushing away the thoughts of Kent. 'How old are you?

'Thirty-one. It's a long time since I played up in the back seat of the school bus.'

'Pease tell me not with my brother.'

'No, Braden only ever had eyes for Julia.'

Kim and Sophie exchanged a sad look. Kim had been part of the group of friends who had supported Braden when Julia died. That's when

Sophie had become friends with Kim, even though she was six years younger than her.

'So what's tonight's function?' Sophie asked as the bus pulled up at the gate and they hurried down the front path.

Kim looked at her sideways. 'A fundraiser. You'll find out when we get there, but trust me, it's going to be a blast. Are you ready for Easter in Augathella?'

Chapter 3

The fundraiser.
Wilson Creek Station
Kent

'How the hell did you ever rope me into this, Ben?' Kent Mason sat in the small shed at the back of the makeshift stage and put his head in his hands. His stomach churned and he was worried he was going to throw up.

Ben Riley, his mate from high school days chuckled. 'There's no need to be nervous, mate. We've got this down pat. And it's for a good cause. The least we can do is contribute.'

'You always were a show pony at school.'

'Ha, thanks for that. Give me credit for a bit of talent. Once we get going you'll be fine. Trust me, you'll enjoy yourself.'

'I know I should have worn a mask. I still could. I think there's one in the glovebox of my ute from the New Year's Eve do. No one will know it's me then.'

'You mean a full mask? I thought you meant a COVID mask. How are you going to sing in a mask?'

'How am I going to sing when I'm shit-scared with nerves?

'Just follow my lead.'

'It sounds like there are thousands out there.'

'I think we're into the hundreds.' Ben opened the door of the shed a chink and peered through. 'The two front rows are filled with strangers. Must be the grey nomies camping at the bore.'

'I can cope with them. They don't know me. Jeez, Ben why I ever agreed to this, I'll never know. I'm sorry you ever came back to town.'

'That makes two of us, mate. Anyway, nerves are a sign of a good performer. If you weren't nervous I'd be worried. All you have to do is perform as well as you did when we practised at my place and you'll be fine.'

Kent took a deep shuddering breath and Ben frowned.

'You really are worked up, aren't you?'

'Duh, quick off the mark, mate.'

'Okay, what are you worried about exactly?'

'That I'll open my mouth and nothing comes out? That I'll forget the words? That I'll forget how to play my guitar? Is that enough? This is a big first for me. It's okay for you, you've been doing it in Brisbane where no one knows you. Hell, man, I grew up with half the people out there!'

'So did I. And they're gonna love you. They're gonna love us! You said no one has a clue that you play and sing?'

'No. Up until you came back to town, it was something I always did at home by myself.'

'Well, that was a waste. You're going to be a huge hit with the locals tonight and they're going to dig deep and donate for the school.'

'And then it will be all over and I can enjoy the rest of the weekend.'

Ben shook his head.

'You know I'd rather be out in the yards facing a cranky bull than doing this.' He stared at Ben. 'What did you mean that makes two of us. I was thinking how lucky you were to get an engineering job on the council here.'

'Nope. I put down all of the major towns from Brisbane to Cairns on my application. The last thing I wanted was to come home to the outback.'

'And here was I thinking how lucky you were. Got a girl on the coast? Is that why you didn't want to come back?'

'No, I wanted to prove to myself somewhere I wasn't known. Here I'm Johnny Riley's son, and I'm accepted for that. Not for the job I do. Plus the old guys on the shire have been there forever and I'm getting all the shit jobs.'

'Can't be that bad.'

'Trust me, how many other shire engineers would have been roped in to do the council dog obedience classes?'

Kent felt a bit better as he laughed. 'Dog obedience classes? I didn't even know they had them.'

'Yep and yours truly is running the show, for frig's sake.'

'I—' Kent held his guitar tightly and widened his eyes as the noise outside quietened and the PA system crackled.

'G'day, folks. A special welcome to our campers who've joined us tonight and a big welcome to the locals who've come all this way from town. Thanks to Jim Anderson for lending us the buses. It's for a good cause, and tonight we're raising money for our local school.' Craig Wilson's voice boomed into the small shed. 'There's a great night planned, but before we introduce our special entertainment—and I know you're going to love these guys—Bob, our principal and Jon Ingram are sitting over at the table to my left and taking entries for the hundred club. Five dollars a number. Come on over. Fallon and Cheryl are at the other table and they're selling tickets for the huge Easter raffle.'

Kent closed his eyes and took a deep breath. Maybe the crowd would be more interested in the winning tickets than the entertainment.

Craig's voice got louder. 'Sophie, can you help Kim carry the basket up so we can show the crowd the size of the raffle prize? Thanks, ladies A big thanks to the local pub who donated all the chocolate eggs.'

'Shit, that's all I need. Sophie's here.'

'Of course, she is. The whole town's turned up. It's the start of a big weekend. Now pull yourself together. Craig said ten minutes for ticket selling and then we're on.'

Kent hugged his guitar close and focused on his breathing.

Chapter 4

Sophie took one end of the giant basket, smiling as she and Kim negotiated the four steps up to the stage.

'There's enough chocolate in here to sink a boat,' Kim said with a grin.

The buzz of the crowd and the happy faces had put Sophie in a good mood. The sun was gone and now it was a clear still night; the wind had dropped and the stars sparkled in an indigo sky. The enticing aroma of frying onions and streak drifted over from the Lions van. Sophie caught Braden's eye and he grinned at her as she and Kimberley held the basket up. Her brother was standing at the back of the seated area with his arm around Callie. The three boys were running around the grass with most of the student population of the primary school. A buoyant mood filled the area and Kimberley smiled at her as she nodded towards the queue forming to buy raffle tickets.

'Looks like they're in the mood to buy.' Craig and his workers had set up a bar next to the hot food van. Some of the crowd had brought their own eskies, but there was a good queue at the bar too, a couple of kegs enticing thirsty patrons.

'Nothing like beer on tap,' Sophie said.

'And less mess,' Kim added. 'Come on. We'll leave this on the stage. If we put it to the left side at the front, it won't get in the way.'

'So what's this mystery entertainment tonight?' Sophie asked as they carried the basket to the side of the raised platform, placing it down carefully on the timber floor.

'Apparently a very good duo. I don't know much about it, Bob was pretty close-mouthed. Said it was to be a surprise.'

'Let's go grab a drink, and find a good seat where we can see what's happening.'

Kim nodded, following Sophie down the stairs. As they neared the grassy area, Braden called out to Sophie and beckoned her over.

'I'll catch up with you, Kim,' Sophie said. 'Can you grab me a beer please? I'll get the next one. I want to have a quick word with Braden.'

'Sure. I'll get us seats as close to the front as possible. Then we can get up and dance.'

'I can't see them having a mosh pit here. Or like that concert you took me to in Longreach when I was just legal!' Sophie rolled her eyes. 'No chance of that, these days, Kim. I hate drawing attention to myself.'

Kim grinned at her. 'Girlfriend in that bodysuit and jeans, you've already got the attention of every red-blooded male from here to Charleville.'

'Well. If they look at my face, they'll see a bit of *not interested*.'

'Famous last words, Sophie.'

Chapter 5

Sophie

'Hey, big brother.' Sophie made her way through the happy crowd and pecked Braden on the cheek. 'What are you looking so pleased about?'

'Nothing in particular. It's a great night, we had thirty ml of rain at the station yesterday and I'm taking Easter off.'

Sophie raised her eyebrows. 'That'll be a first.'

'Not really. It's just these past few months I've been working hard. Making up for all those months when I was a mess. Now life's settled, and there's only one thing that would make it better.'

'And what would that be?' she asked suspiciously, knowing exactly what he was going to say.

'I've thought about what you said. Will you come out and help me?'

'When?'

Braden put his hand up. 'As soon as possible?' He took her arm and they walked over near the fence where it was quieter. Sophie folded her arms. She really didn't have a decent argument.

'Ever since Kent and I brought you back, you've avoided coming home. You've only been out to visit once.'

'I'm coming out tomorrow to get something to wear to the races on Monday.'

'And then where are you going to stay? I know Celia is coming to stay with Kim for Easter.'

Sophie shrugged. 'I haven't decided yet.'

'I can't understand why you just won't say yes. You can stay in our side of the house. Is it because of Callie? Or have I done something to upset you?'

Sophie bit her lip as a myriad of feelings churned through her. How could she tell Braden what was wrong? *She* didn't even know what the matter was.

Okay, so she was embarrassed at getting sucked in by Jock and agreeing to move away from all she loved. She was doubly embarrassed that she had let Jock treat her the way he had for so long.

And it was doubly awkward that Kent had been one of her rescuers when she'd called Braden for help. The last thing she'd expected was to see his plane turn up, although to have Braden climb out and open his arms to her had made it bearable. She had felt safe.

'I like Callie. A lot. You're great together and I'm really pleased to see you both so happy. And the boys too.' She gestured over to the lawn where the three of them were playing with the other kids. 'Look how happy they are.'

'We're talking about you, Soph. I'm worried about you. Do you need to go and see someone?'

'See someone? Like who?'

'You know someone to talk to, After what you went through with Jock. Not that you've told me.' He looked her square in the eye. 'You need to talk to someone.'

'No. I *don't*. I handled it. And I got out. A lot of women don't. And you're a fine one to talk. You didn't go and talk to "*someone*" when everyone said you needed to.'

'Everyone?'

'Well, me. I did.'

'We're a fine pair, Soph. We've never been much good at knowing how to deal with *stuff*.' Braden moved closer to her. 'I'm just trying to help. I'm worried about you . . . please come home to *Kilcoy Station*. We all want you there. Me, and Callie, and the boys. I was serious about you taking the cooking on. If you do, I'll put you on the payroll. If you don't, I'll have to hire someone. I've got a team of new young ringers moving into the old sheds. We've got a busy winter season ahead.'

Sophie relaxed her shoulders and stared at her brother for a long moment. 'All right, but on one condition.'

'Anything you ask for!'

'Seeing the dongas are full, you and I will sort out the other side of the house. I'll stay in the closed-up section of the house to give you and Callie and the boys your privacy. And I'll do it for three months only.'

'And then what?'

'And then I'm escaping.'

'Escaping?' His eyebrows rose.

'Leaving, spot on three months. I feel trapped here, Bray. Everyone is looking at me and feeling sorry for me, but they don't say anything. Kim talked me into coming here tonight and to the races. I didn't want to.'

'And the rodeo and the billy cart race, I hope. Rory and Nigel have entered the under-nines. You should see the cart. Callie's done it in a rainbow theme.' Braden shook his head and stared at her. 'And where are you going if you leave? What are you going to do?' He ran a hand through his hair and she could see the worry etched on his face. Guilt tugged at her, but determination won.

'I don't know. I'll sort something. Look, the show's about to start. I'll come out early tomorrow and get organised. We'll talk more then.'

'Okay, Soph. Thank you. I owe you and . . .'

'And what?'

Braden cleared his throat and shuffled his feet. 'And . . . I love you, sis.'

Sophie swallowed and stared at him. She stood on her toes and brushed a kiss on her brother's cheek. 'I love you too, you big galoot.' She put her head down and walked away. For Braden to show her affection like that was a huge step. They'd not been a demonstrative family when their parents had been alive, and over the last few years, Sophie had come to realise what a sterile family life she and Braden had growing up.

Callie had been so good for Braden; tonight was the first time in their lives that he had shown Sophie spontaneous brotherly affection like that. She was still hesitant about moving to the station, but she knew Braden needed her; the more she thought about it, the more she realised it would be good to have her own space. She hadn't had that since they'd moved out of the original farmhouse that the station manager, Jon, and his partner, Fallon, lived in now.

As long as Braden could deal with her living in the side of the house where he and Julia and the boys had lived before Julia had been killed in the accident.

'Over here, Sophie.'

Sophie turned at Kim's call. Her friend was standing on a chair in the second row from the front of the stage and was waving at her.

'Quick, the show's about to start,' she said.

The mood of the crowd buzzed with anticipation as a spotlight lit up the centre of the stage where someone had placed two stools. A bank of amplifiers and sound gear sat behind a huge basket of Easter eggs at the side of the stage.

Sophie checked out the crowd as she hurried along the narrow walkway between the two sections of chairs; she was surprised to see that every chair was filled. To the left and right of each block of plastic chairs, families had spread picnic rugs and set up camp chairs on the grass. She smiled as she recognised some of her friends from school, not that she'd made many in the one year she went to the local high school. Once she'd met Kent they had pretty much been an item and hadn't spent a lot of time in the social group. It had been an idyllic year for her. For the first time in her eighteen years, she'd felt valued . . . and loved.

Now her current friendship group was made up of people Braden had become friends with over the years and they were all older than she was. Most of her friends were married now and already had kids. Some had moved away but she still kept in touch by email.

Maybe in the future she'd move to a town where she knew someone already. Sophie pulled a face as she reached the row where Kim was sitting. No, she would be independent and she'd find somewhere to move to where she could make a fresh start. No history, and no one who knew what poor choices she'd made. She'd escape this country town and the memories and she'd find a job in a totally new place.

But what sort of job?

Although Sophie had completed high school, she knew she had no special skills and little experience in the workforce. Even though she'd never finished her course, she could cook, so maybe she could move to a station in a different district. She made a note to start looking online for jobs.

Maybe she could move north.

No! She dismissed that idea immediately. Nope, nowhere near Jock. It would suit her if she never laid eyes on Jock Evans again. A shiver ran down her spine and she blocked the memories. She had been so naive.

'Sophie, hurry up! Stop daydreaming and come and sit down.' Kim was three seats along the row and had her bag minding the seat beside her.

'Okay, I'm coming I'm coming.' Sophie stood at the end of the row. 'Excuse me.'

The three people in the seats at the end of the row moved their legs sideways and held their drinks close to their chest as Sophie pushed through. In the front row in front, the mayor sat beside his wife but she didn't recognise the others with them.

'Quick, Soph. Sit down it's about to start. Here's your drink.' Kim pointed to the stage where an attractive young woman in a red dress and high heels stood holding the microphone. 'Look. Even a proper MC. Jacinta has done a great job.'

'Who is that?' Sophie said. 'Someone I should know?'

'No. Apparently, she's the announcer at the new ABC radio station. I haven't met her yet.'

'So Craig got her to do the honours to introduce this mystery duo.' Sophie settled back in the chair and took a sip of her beer. They had a fine view of the stage.

Kim looked at her. 'Um, Soph? I haven't been quite honest with you. I actually do know who it is but I didn't want to tell you because I didn't think you'd come.'

'Why not?' Sophie frowned. 'Why wouldn't I have come. I know I'm not a big country and western music fan, but it's for a good cause.'

'Um, you'll see soon.' Kim pulled a face.

The PA system hummed and the pretty woman spoke into the microphone. 'Good evening, ladies and gentlemen. I'm Mel from your local ABC station.'

A huge cheer went up.

'Thank you. It's fabulous to be here for the first function to kick off the Augathella Easter events. A huge thank you to Craig and Mandy Wilson for letting us use their station for the concert tonight. I'm really looking forward to getting to know you all. It's a fabulous fundraiser tonight, so dig deep and let's make a difference for the local primary school. I'm sure we're going to see lots of students in the billy cart races on Sunday. But without further ado, let's get this music on the road. We've got a special duo for you and I'm sure you're going to enjoy the music of "*The Augie Boys*". Please put your hands together and settle back for some great music.'

Sophie rolled her eyes. '"*The Augie Boys*"? It's someone local?'

Kim nodded and took a swig of her beer in the plastic cup. 'Sure is. It's Ben Riley and you'll see who else in a minute. So prepare yourself.'

Sophie had no idea why she'd have to prepare herself. She didn't know anyone local who sang or played music. The only semi-local musicians she'd ever seen at the pub had come from Charleville, plus there was a band from Tambo who had come through a few times when she and Kent had still been at school. He'd loved his music and was always playing something new for her. He'd introduced her to soft rock. Art rock, he'd called it back then. Kent had done music for his final exams, but she'd never seen him play an instrument.

Or sing.

Suspicion crept into her thoughts, and she shook her head.

Surely not?

The stage lights went out and the crowd quietened as the MC stepped off the stage. Plaintive guitar notes broke the silence, and the lights gradually began to come back on, until a spotlight now illuminated the two stools that had previously been empty.

Two guys in black jeans, black T-shirts and dark Akubras sat on the stools. The spotlight shone on them but they both had their heads down as the one on the right began to pluck the guitar strings. The music was beautiful and as she watched, spellbound, the guy on the left sat straight and lifted a harmonica to his lips. The music he made was magic.

Relief filled Sophie for a second, but it disappeared instantly as the second musician lifted his head and Kent Mason's eyes looked her way. For a moment she thought he was looking at her and then the woman sitting in front of her jumped up and waved madly.

'Go, Kent!' Jennifer Shaw screamed out.

Sophie let out a gasp and stared as Kent began to sing.

Kent?

It was his voice, but it was strong and true and perfectly in tune as he launched into her favourite Chris Isaac song. He had the most beautiful voice. Dismay filled her as he shared his hidden talent with most of Augathella.

'You okay, Soph? Bit of a surprise packet, hey?'

Sophie gave a brief nod, aware of Kim looking at her, but *she* was having trouble taking her eyes off Kent.

Chapter 6

Kent

Once they'd been introduced by the ABC announcer and they'd started their performance, Kent managed to switch off and ignore the crowd in front of the stage. He looked out over the faceless people and the velvet sky as pinpricks of stars began to appear above.

He and Ben were good together; he knew that. The sound system with the microphones and the amplifiers made them sound even better. Their voices harmonised well, and Ben was a gun on the harmonica. They played a set of six songs, back to back, and he didn't stumble on one word or one note. By the time they were singing the last chorus of the final song of the set, Kent was relaxed and enjoying himself.

As they wound it up, Ben gestured to Rusty Wilson, Craig's eighteen-year-old son, who was in charge of the lighting. Rusty was doing a great job, and on the last note of the song as their voices lowered to diminuendo, the stage plunged into darkness. As Ben and Kent exited through the back curtain and headed to the shed behind the stage for a break and a cold drink, the applause from the crowd and the calls for "more, more" was deafening.

Ben opened the door and Kent followed him into the small space. Ben held up his hand and they high-fived each other.

Euphoria flooded through Kent and the feeling was better than the high of soaring in the sky in his twin-engine Cessna.

'Told ya, mate. We blitzed it.' Ben paced around the small space as Kent went to the esky and grabbed two beers. He'd drunk three bottles of water on stage. He shook his head.

'Why was I so nervous? There wasn't any need to be, was there?'

'Because you take pride in your work. And are you for real? You've never performed live before? With a talent like yours!'

'Never. It's just something I've done for myself. Not even my sister knew I could sing until tonight.' Kent chuckled. 'I sing when I'm out in the paddocks. The cattle could tell some stories.'

'I'm mighty pleased that I heard you that night.'

Kent had been sitting at the back of his house strumming his guitar and singing one night a few weeks ago, not long after he'd flown Braden up to collect Sophie. He'd been feeling a bit unsettled, wondering why he hadn't been enough for her and how she'd ended up with that bastard, Jock Evans instead. He'd put his feelings into his strumming and singing, and hadn't heard Ben arrive, and the first he knew, Ben had pulled out his harmonica and was improvising beside him.

'We make a good team. I reckon we'll be asked to do some pub and club gigs after this. Are you up for it?' Ben swigged a can of beer in one hit.

'Really?'

'Yeah, once Mel interviews us, the word will spread. You on?'

'You're jumping the gun a bit, Ben, I'd say.' Kent was cautious in everything he did, but he couldn't help the grin pulling at his lips. 'If it does happen, I reckon I could find the time.'

'Let's go out and mingle with the crowd. You never know our luck. There are a lot of single women out there. A man might get lucky tonight.'

Kent grinned. 'You go mingle. I'm going to sit here and catch my breath for a while.'

***

'Another beer, Soph?'

'Huh?' Sophie came out of her daze. How come she hadn't known Kent could sing? He had the voice of an angel. And how hot did he look on that stage in his black outfit? She pushed away the feeling; she had no right to react like that, and she didn't want to anyway. Every woman from zero to ninety in the crowd would be salivating over Kent

Mason tonight. He looked like a rock star, and more to the point he'd sounded like one too.

'Do you want another beer? We might as well, seeing as we're getting the bus home.' Kim yelled over the noise of the crowd.

Sophie jumped to her feet, finally gathering her wits. 'You stay there. My shout. Do you want some hot chips?'

'No, but I could go a steak sanga.'

Kim stayed on her feet. 'I'll grab the drinks and you get in the food queue. Steak sanga for you too?'

'Yes, I should eat.' Sophie wasn't very hungry but she knew she needed something to soak up the beer.

She made her way to the food tent and joined the food queue. A tap on her shoulder had her turning around.

'Hey, Sophie!' Callie held her arms open. 'I am so pleased you're coming home. Braden told me you'd agreed. I could barely sit still I was so happy. And you've made *his* night.'

Sophie wasn't sure what to say as she hugged Callie. Even though she'd agreed, she still wasn't sure it was the right decision. But since she'd sat there listening to Kent sing, her head wasn't in the right space to try and think about the next few months so she simply smiled at Callie.

Callie was on a high. 'And how good were Kent and Ben? Even with all the live outdoor concerts I went to in Brissie, I've never heard such a great performance.'

'Ben?' Sophie asked. 'I thought I recognised him. Was that Ben Riley?'

'Braden said it was a Ben he went to school with. I don't know his last name.'

Sophie nodded. 'It *was* Ben Riley. Fair dinkum, the night is full of surprises.'

'But what a great night. The boys are so excited. Are you coming to the billy cart races on Sunday?'

'Wouldn't miss it for the world.'

'And the races on Monday?'

'Yes, and the races.' Sophie couldn't help her smile. 'I have a reputation to uphold.'

'And the rodeo tomorrow? Braden's expecting the new jillaroo to arrive in town and he told her we'd be there. When do you think you'll come home?'

Sophie thought quickly. 'I haven't decided, but maybe I'll come out tomorrow. I've got the dinner shift at the pub. I'm not sure if it'll be busy after the rodeo or not.'

'There are a lot of tourists in town for Easter, so I'd say it might be. The two motels and the caravan park are full, and a lot of campers out here at Craig's.'

Sophie smiled at Callie. 'You sound like you've got to know the town very well. I know you're happy out at *Kilcoy Station,* but it must be very different to Brisbane.'

The queue moved forward a little.

Callie nodded slowly. 'When I came out here, I had no idea what I was coming to. Even the long drive out was a first for me. I encountered my first dust storm, and I had no idea about living on the land. I'm sure Braden thought I was a fool.'

'He got over that quickly if he did. So you've settled? No homesickness for the city?'

'No. I'm here to stay. I've contacted my friend Jen. She's going to property manage my house for me while I rent it out. Braden and I are going to go back to Brisbane before school goes back. I want to show him some of my furniture. It'll fill up some of the empty spaces in the house.'

Sophie hesitated. 'Has Braden showed you the other side of the house yet?'

'No. And I haven't pushed. We've been busy with me going into town to school. I know he finds it hard. Of course, he does. And that's why I'm not sharing his bedroom. You know, when I headed out here, I had no idea how life would turn out for me. I'm still not rushing into anything. I've only been out here six months.'

Sophie put her hands up. 'That's between you and Braden, Callie.'

'Sophie, you're family, and I'm very conscious of not pushing in. As much as I love Braden, I think we need to take things slow. Our relationship affects others, including you. I'm here to stay— if Braden wants me to.'

'I have no doubt of that, Callie. My brother has mellowed a lot since you arrived, and it's clear that he loves you too.'

Even in the dim light Sophie saw the blush rise into Callie's cheeks. Even though she came across as really confident, maybe Callie held the same fears and worries that she did too.

'One word of advice, Callie. Be careful. Don't risk your love by doubting, and not talking. Often there's no going back. I still don't know whether I'll hang around here. I'm thinking about moving away in a while.'

'I'm sorry to hear that, and I'm sorry about your relationship breaking up.'

'Which one?' Sophie frowned, wondering what Braden had told Callie.

'You and Jock.'

'God no. Don't be sorry about that. That was a mistake on the rebound. I was talking about the past. Way before Jock.'

The microphone crackled on the stage and Sophie looked up anxiously. She wanted to be back in her seat before Kent and Ben started singing again. 'Gosh, this food queue is slow. I feel like getting in the van and helping them!'

'We've got time. It's a thirty-minute break. Braden asked Craig what the program was,' Callie said, with a slight shake of her head. 'I think Craig's going to do the raffle ticket sales spiel now.'

Sure enough, Craig's voice boomed over the mike. 'Come and get your tickets. Don't miss out. Look at this fabulous prize. The biggest basket of chocolate you'll find anywhere in the Murweh Shire. I've also heard that there's a new second prize, young ladies. A mystery date with one of the fellas up here on stage. I wonder which one it is?' Craig grinned as there was a rush of young women to the raffle ticket table.

'You'll have to buy some tickets, Sophie,' Callie said.

'Nuh.' Sophie shook her head. 'I'm over dates, mystery or otherwise, for life.'

'Well, at least you can enjoy the music. Braden told me Ben's a local too.'

'Yeah, I went to school with Ben. His parents have a wheat property not far out of town, and his mum is a dog breeder. I was surprised when he came back. He always swore he was going to move away.'

'I'm glad he's here. They sing so well together, and Kent's a whizz on the guitar. They're so good! I'm having the best time.'

'They are.' Sophie didn't let on how surprised she was by Kent's presence up there; she didn't really want to talk about him. She reached over and looped her arm through Callie's. 'I know I've been a bit preoccupied since I got home, but I want you to know I'm really happy that you and Bray are together. And I do hope we can be good friends.'

'Thank you, Sophie. That means a lot. I hope we can be friends too. Fallon and I have already hit it off. I couldn't believe it when she and Jon crashed in that dust storm.'

'She must be a damn good pilot.'

'Braden said she's the best. Did you know she and Jon are having a baby now? It's great that they've moved into the house at the back of your station. Having Jon there gives Braden more time to spend with the boys.'

The man under discussion strode across the grass to stand with them. Sophie saw the minute Braden noticed that she had her arm looped through Callie's and his expression changed to one of deep satisfaction.

'What's the hold up with the food?' he asked. 'I'm starving and the boys are making noises about hot chips and icy poles.'

'It smells so good, even the families who brought a picnic have lined up for a steak. More money for the school,' Callie said. 'I've got a big order. I know the appetites of those three little men. But I didn't think of icy poles. They'll probably melt.'

'Grab three,' Braden said. 'I'll put them in the esky with the beer and the ice.'

Sophie met her brother's gaze and he smiled at her as he mouthed 'thank you' above Callie's head.

Chapter 7

Kent

Ten minutes before they were due to go back on stage, Kent decided he needed to find some food. Since they'd stopped playing, the adrenaline had dissipated and he knew he needed an energy hit if they were going to play for another two hours. The appetising aroma of steak and onions had drifted across and his stomach grumbled. He stood and put his guitar at the back of the stage.

Kent knew he was the opposite of Ben. The last thing he wanted to do was put on a performance as the star of the show. He was embarrassed enough about performing in front of people who knew him, but he knew they'd done good, and there was nothing to be embarrassed about. He grabbed his black Akubra and plonked it on firmly, putting his head down as he left the shed and headed for the Lions' van.

So far, so good. He moved through a crowd of unfamiliar faces, and no one called out to him. As he joined the back of the queue at the van, he looked up and encountered his first familiar face.

And of course, it had to be Sophie Cartwright.

She was walking towards him carrying a couple of steak burgers wrapped in white paper, and a bucket of hot chips. Uncertainty crossed her face and Kent knew she was weighing up whether to keep walking, or stop and acknowledge that she'd seen him. He took the choice away from her.

'Hey, Soph,' he called out. 'I didn't know you were here. Not working at the pub tonight?'

In fact, he had been hoping she wasn't here. But at least he hadn't made a fool of himself.

'*Act normal,*' he whispered under his breath.

'No.' Despite her one-word reply, Sophie did stop beside him. Her eyes held his and he ignored that kick to his heart that had never gone away.

The silence lengthened and became awkward. 'You sing very well,' she finally said. 'I didn't know you could, Kent.'

Okay, if she could play it normal, so could he.

'I'm sure there were a lot of things we didn't know about each other.' Hurt laced his words, but Kent refused to lash out. No matter how much Sophie had hurt him by her actions, and despite his resolution never to forget how much he'd been hurt—that kept his heart safe—he knew if he said what he was feeling, it would turn into a blue. Kent had buried his hurt and kept his distance when Sophie had moved in with Jock.

When Jock had come to see him and told him that he and Sophie were in love with each other but she wouldn't go public because she didn't want to hurt Kent's feelings, Kent had laughed in his face.

'You're living in dreamland, mate,' he'd said. 'I'd advise you to stay away from my Soph if you want to keep out of trouble.'

Jock Evans was a show pony and had been out with most of the single women in the district in the six months since he'd hit town and started work at Jack Anderson's garage. He didn't settle with anyone; it was a well-known fact he was a user, and he'd got into a bit of trouble at the pub a few weeks back and had been banned for fighting.

Jock's eyes had been as hard as steel. 'Maybe you should ask Sophie.'

'I wouldn't insult her by doing that,' Kent had replied.

'You're in for a fall then, mate.' Jock had taken a step closer, but Kent had held his ground.

Kent and Sophie had been a couple since high school, but since his parents had semi-retired and left the management of *Lara Waters* to him, they had seen less of each other. His sister, Jacinta, wasn't interested in the station, and worked at the school in town. Sophie was at TAFE in Charleville through the week at her hospitality course, and for two months back then, Kent had been busy most weekends, mustering and supervising the ringers.

Sophie helped Julia out with her three small nephews when he was working weekends. Two weeks after Jock had bailed him up, Sophie had come to see Kent and told him she was breaking up with him, he'd been heartbroken. The fact that she wouldn't say why worried him, and he'd spent many sleepless hours trying to figure out what he'd done. *Why* she'd broken up with him, and *why* had she turned to Jock Evans of all people.

I loved her. And I thought she loved me.

Maybe he'd been too complacent and taken for granted that Sophie knew he'd fully intended they would marry in the future and run *Lara Waters* together. Maybe his communication skills had been lacking. Maybe he should have shown her how much he loved her. Maybe he had taken her for granted.

When Sophie moved in with Jock Evans only a couple of weeks later, Kent vowed never to trust a woman again. How could she have thrown away what they had? They'd spent so long together, enjoyed being together, and they'd been a couple. No reason, no explanation. A part of Kent died that day, and he'd vowed he would never give his heart again, even if it meant turning into a cranky old guy like Fallon's uncle, George Malone.

It had been so hard to stay away from Sophie when only a few days later Julia had died in a horse accident at *Kilcoy Station*, and the boys had soon moved to Jock and Sophie's place.

Now the woman he had once loved stood right in front of him, her voice cold, and her eyes almost shooting icicles at him.

Where had his warm and lovely Sophie gone?

Maybe she had just been a manifestation of his imagination. Maybe he'd only seen what he wanted to, and now she was showing what she was really like. 'Perhaps there was, Kent. And one of the things I didn't know was how mean you are when things don't go your way. Just remember you brought it all on yourself.'

'Mean?' He stared at her as she grabbed for the chips as they started to slip from her grip.

'Yes, mean,' she hissed. 'The look on your face now says it all. I don't think I can sit there any longer and hear you sing bloody love songs. You are such a fraud.'

Kent's mouth dropped open as Sophie turned on her heel and strode away. His appetite had vanished and he turned and walked back to the shed behind the stage. That was the most he and Sophie had ever talked about their breakup since the day she'd left him two years ago.

What had she meant by saying he'd brought it all on himself?

'You ready to go again?' Ben was inside holding a beer as Kent pushed the door open.

Stuff her, he'd sing all the love songs he wanted to, and he'd sing them bloody well.

'Let's go get 'em,' Kent said, determined to show Sophie that he could ignore her nasty words.

'I've created a monster.' Ben slapped him on the back as they headed for the stage.

Chapter 8

Two years earlier

It had taken less than a month before Sophie suspected she had made a mistake moving in with Jock. By that time, Julia's accident had rocked their world and they'd somehow survived the funeral and all that went with it; their lives had changed. Sophie had tried to support Braden as best she could. Kent had been amazing and had moved into the house with Braden to field phone calls and visitors while Sophie coped with three little boys who had lost their mother. They had managed to be civil to each other; the circumstances called for no less.

But the closeness they once shared was in the past. Jock had agreed for the boys to come and live at the station they were now managing—his job had only lasted six months at the local garage.

'Of course, they can come and stay with us. I love the little tykes. They might as well be here, otherwise, I'll never see you,' he'd said. 'But you know you'll have to give up your course at Charleville. You can't expect me to take up the slack for you.'

'Take up the slack for me?' Sophie had questioned him the night before she was going to collect the boys, her eyes wide. She'd come back to their place for one night because Jock had asked her to, but all she'd done was worry about Rory, Nigel and baby Petie.

'They're your rellies, and anyway, I'm sick of coming home to an empty house and having to cook my own meals after a day out in the paddocks. The accident happened at a good time. It's woken you up to yourself about doing this course. Waste of time. You can get a job anywhere around here without needing a certificate to say you can do it. Braden can put in a good word for you. I said I'd give you some time, but it's time for you to start pulling your weight around here. I'm not a charity.'

Sophie had stared at him, and too upset to talk, she'd disappeared into her bedroom. The manager's house on this station was a dump, and she sat on the side of the hard bed and squeezed her eyes shut to stop the tears coming.

The accident had happened at a good time! Had he really said that? How could he?

She hadn't told anyone about the letter that had arrived the morning of Julia's death. A letter offering her a scholarship to finish her Certificate IV in Commercial Cookery working in a restaurant on the Brisbane River with Damon Dean, one of

Brisbane's top chefs. She had already known that living with Jock wasn't going to work out, and had decided to take the offer.

Before Sophie could think any more about what she'd given up, Jock had opened the door.

'I'm so sorry, Soph. That came out the wrong way. You know me. I'm not real good with words. I'm an insensitive bastard, not good enough for you. I'm sorry. I do care about you, Soph.'

His arms had gone around her, and she'd stood rigid in his grip. She wasn't ready for a relationship and he knew that. They were all on edge; grief did awful things to the way you thought and spoke. She had to stay now; the boys needed her, and she needed a home where she could look after them. Jock had agreed, and she had to make the best of the situation. If only Kent hadn't spoiled everything.

It could have been she and Kent helping Braden out. Sophie had pushed those thoughts away and the next morning she drove across to *Kilcoy Station*. Taking a deep breath, trying to be strong to talk to Braden, she stepped out of the car and made her way to the back door. Kent had been waiting there.

'The boys are in the living room, I've got the TV on. Petie's had a bottle and he's happy on the floor.'

'Where's Braden?'

'He's still asleep. He had a bit too much to drink last night.'

'Again?' Sophie moved around the kitchen tidying up. Anything not to meet Kent's eyes.

'Yes. It's a good thing you,'—he hesitated slightly—'and Jock are doing for Braden, Soph. Take the boys away for a couple of weeks; it'll give him a chance to get back on an even keel. Don't worry, I'll keep a close eye on him. You just look after the little ones. Nigel's been crying all morning and asking for Mummy.' The whole time he was speaking their eyes didn't meet.

'Poor baby.' For a moment, Sophie wanted to lean into Kent and have him hold her and comfort her, and then she remembered what he'd done. Her eyes welled as she realised she needed to thank him for helping Braden in the past week. She swallowed back the lump in her throat. 'Thanks, Kent. You've been a great help.'

He'd shrugged. 'Braden's my best mate. Of course I was here for him. He said last night for you to take the boys home with you and he'd come out and see them later in the week. He doesn't want to see you this morning. He's not in a good place. I'll stay here with him for the day.'

Tears ran down Sophie's face and when she'd looked up, Kent had been staring at her, his eyes full of sadness. Again, all she wanted to do was crawl into his arms and let him hold her until everything was better.

No matter what.

Life was too short; they should have talked about what had happened. Maybe she could have forgiven him.

But now she straightened her shoulders, reminding herself that what he had done had been *unforgivable*. Okay, so she'd loved him once, but Kent was here for Braden now, not for *her*.

Sophie knew she had to grow up, grow strong and learn to deal with things. She forced herself to remember that things had changed. She couldn't cling to the past.

She had to look to the future, and consider the welfare of her three nephews.

As she packed the car and drove out with the boys in the back, she had no idea it would be two years before they went home again.

Chapter 9

The fundraiser.
Wilson Creek Station
Sophie

Kim grinned up at Sophie as she made her way along the narrow row between the seats.

'Excuse me. Sorry, sorry.' Sophie apologised as she trod on booted feet, knocking one can of beer flying as she pushed along to the seat beside Kim. The smell of spilled beer mingled with frying onions and the appetising aroma of the hot chips she carried.

'I thought you must have been peeling the spuds,' Kim said reaching for the chips. 'I'm starving.'

'There was a queue a mile long. Listen, are you okay if I leave you here and go look after my nephews?'

'Sure. It's been non-stop chat here. Half the school staff are in these two rows.'

'It'll give Braden and Callie a chance to have a dance.'

'I just want you to have a good time, Soph. Are you going to eat first?'

Before Sophie could answer the stage lights came on, and Craig took the microphone.

'A big round of applause, the Augie Boys are back!'

A loud guitar riff filled the air and Sophie raised her voice to be heard. 'Nuh. I'm not hungry anymore.' She stood and reached for her bag. 'I'll go out this way. Fewer feet to tread on. I'll see you on the bus later.'

'Are you okay?' Kim's eyes narrowed.

'Yeah, why?'

'No reason. You don't seem very happy.'

'I'm fine. Just a bit preoccupied. I've had a chat with Braden, and I'm going to move out to *Kilcoy Station* tomorrow. It'll give you space for you and your sisters to have a good catch-up.'

'It's fine if you want to stay. We can make room.'

'No, it's time I went home. I'll strip my bed and wash the towels for you in the morning.'

'You don't have to do all that. We'll have a yak on the bus on the way home.'

'Okay. I'll see you in a while. I'll meet you out where the buses are when it's over. Enjoy the entertainment.'

Sophie put her head down and made her way along the row, aware of Kim's curious expression as she crossed to the grassed area where the boys were playing chase with a few kids from school.

There was already a crowd on the flat area in front of the stage, but Callie and Braden were sitting in the back row. Braden sat sideways in the plastic chair at the end of the row keeping a close eye on his three sons.

Sophie walked over and put her hand on her brother's shoulder. 'I'll watch the boys for you. You pair go and have a dance.'

'You sure?'

'Yeah. It was too noisy for me up the front.'

'Bit of a surprise to see Kent up there, hey sis? Did you know he could play and sing?'

'No, I didn't. Have the boys had their icy poles yet?'

'Yes, they've eaten and they'll play until the end. Then they'll sleep all the way home.'

'Off you go then. Go and show Callie your moves.' Sophie grinned. 'Does she know what a great boot scooter you are?'

Callie leaned over. 'What's boot scooting?'

Braden jumped up and took her hand. 'You don't know what boot scooting is, city girl? Come and I'll teach you. You're in for a treat.'

The look on her brother's face as he led Callie to the front of the stage brought a smile to Sophie's face. She could put up with hearing Kent's singing if it made Braden and Callie happy.

But she didn't have to look at the stage.

##

Sophie watched the boys for a while and then put her head back and looked up at the beautiful night sky. It was a crystal clear night and a myriad of stars sparkled above them in an indigo sky. As she looked, a star shot across the sky.

Sophie smiled. Her mum used to say that a shooting star meant something good was going to happen. Maybe she was going to get a great job as a chef in an exotic location and get away from all the unhappiness here.

Rory and Nigel raced over to her, with Petie not too far behind. 'We're hungry, Aunty Soph.'

'Again?' She dug in the basket that Callie had packed and found enough snacks to keep the boys happy as they sat beside her. Once they were settled, Sophie closed her eyes and listened to the music, and tried to block out that it was Kent singing. Ben was good too, she would focus on his voice.

If she'd known what the night was going to bring, she would have stayed home.

Home? She didn't even have one.

Sophie shook herself mentally. Having words with Kent had left her unsettled, and she was letting things get to her way too much.

An hour and a half later, Braden and Callie came back to where Sophie was sitting. Their cheeks were glowing, but they were both laughing. It was wonderful to see her brother happy, so she shook her morose mood off.

'I can now officially boot scoot, Sophie,' Callie told her with glee.

'And she's a natural,' Braden said.

Despite Braden's expectations that they would play with their friends until late, the three boys had crashed. Petie was curled up in the chair beside Sophie with his head in her lap, and Nigel was on the ground at her feet leaning back against her legs, his chin on his chest.

Rory was still awake in the chair on the other side of her, but his eyes were heavy.

'Time to take these boys home to bed,' Sophie said. 'The music's over, isn't it?'

'Yeah, Craig's just going to draw the raffles and then Jim will get his drivers to bring the buses around. But we might get these boys onto the bus now. There'll be a rush soon.' Braden bent down and scooped Nigel up into his arms. 'Cal, can you get Petie?'

'I can.'

'Rory, you okay to walk, buddy?'

'I'll walk with Auntie Sophie.' A little warm—and sticky—hand crept into hers.

'Did you have fun, Rory?' Sophie asked.

'I had the best time. Did you, Aunty Soph?'

Before she could answer, Craig's voice boomed across the crowd. 'We have raffle winners. Jennifer Shaw has won the Easter basket, and . . . drum roll'—Craig sounded a drum roll into the microphone but it simply sounded like static—'ta-da! The winner of the date with our lead singer, Mr Kent Augie Boy Mason is . . . Sophie Cartwright.'

Chapter 10

Sophie

The Rodeo

The morning had been busy with an early start, and after getting back to town late last night, Sophie was tired. Since Sophie had seen Kent on stage she'd been unsettled. Her sleep had been broken by dreams of Kent sitting up on the stage, singing and shaking his head and pointing at her every time she stood to leave.

After helping Kim with the washing, and tidying the large house, it was too early to go to the billy cart races so she decided to take her things out to *Kilcoy Station*. The closer she got to the property, the more unsettled she felt, even though she knew it was time to go home. She'd hidden away in town long enough. The only comments she'd had from locals when she'd been working at the pub had been a friendly welcome and no one seemed to be judging her about the Jock situation. Her coming home was her business, and no one needed to know why she had. Braden was a different matter, and even though he'd dropped everything and got Kent to fly up to get her as soon as she'd called him, they still hadn't talked about what had happened.

And she didn't want to. She wasn't going to.

Coming back home to Augathella had been the wrong decision, but when Jock had grabbed her and yelled at her, she had come to an instant decision. She had made it clear what their relationship was, but he'd started to touch her before that, and she'd become scared of being in the house with him.

She knew Braden and Kent had seen the bruises on her wrists when they'd come to get her, but they'd said nothing, and she hadn't been in any state to talk. She should have taken herself away from Jock without calling Braden, but when Jock had been violent towards her she had been terrified.

Even though she'd not been happy for a long time, in the past Jock had provided a home for her and the boys. The little ones had kept her busy, as had looking after Jock. He'd agreed to share his house with them and even though he had a short fuse, he'd never once raised a hand to her before. He had, however, isolated her from her family and friends. He always wanted to know where she was going when she went to town, and how long she'd be. She knew she had reason to be grateful to him, but when she'd been so busy with the boys, he had gradually taken control of her, and she hadn't really been aware of it.

Moving such a long way away from Augathella had obviously been a part of his ploy to get what he wanted. When he'd suggested it, she'd reluctantly agreed. She had no reason to stay in her hometown. But she'd also had no interest in a relationship with him, and he'd agreed that they were simply sharing a house.

No ties. No relationship.

She'd fallen for it when he'd told her it would help Braden, and let her brother establish a relationship with his sons without her in the background.

In hindsight, Sophie realised how manipulative Jock had been and how foolish she'd been to agree to move away with him under the guise of a platonic relationship. He'd never had any intention of that. He had been after a share in their station the whole time. She had believed him, but had learned her lesson.

First Kent had lied to her, and then Jock had conned her. Her weakness back then, and her agreeance to move away with Jock disgusted her.

She'd been so gullible. 'Why do we have to go so far? There's plenty of work around here,' she'd asked. Even though it had been time for the boys to go back to Braden, she'd worried about leaving them and not being on call.

'It's a fantastic offer, Sophie. A flash house, a new Landcruiser and a great salary package. And they want a cook too.' Jock had stepped forward to put his arms around her, but she'd moved away. 'A new start away from the past, the grief and sadness, plus it'll give your brother a chance to be a real father to those three little fellas. When he's settled, we can go back and you can take your share in *Kilcoy Station*. Then we can be a real couple.'

She'd pulled away from him. 'We're not a couple, Jock. That was never the deal.'

'But we will be. You know I'm in love with you. I wouldn't have taken those bloody kids on if I hadn't cared about you.'

Now she knew exactly what Jock had cared about.

Money and land.

In hindsight, she'd realised when they lived in Augathella, Jock had known her family home was close enough for her to go back home if he did the wrong thing. It hadn't been until they'd moved north, and Braden was a long way away, that Jock had shown his true colours for the first time.

He'd thought he had her where he wanted her, and she knew he would have been astounded that she was thinking of leaving.

Jock Evans had misread her. She hadn't been in a relationship with him and didn't intend to be.

Sophie knew she had been stupid to move away with him, but she hadn't been thinking straight. Julia's death and Kent's betrayal had messed with her head, and she'd seen the move as a means to get away.

When they'd arrived at the property and the so-called fabulous job at Innot Springs, she had been dismayed. The house wasn't far off being a hovel, there was no car, and no job for her. Jock tried to bluff his way out of it, but she knew he'd been lying all along.

A month after they'd arrived Jock had come home from work early. Sophie had spent the day trying to clean up the house they were living in, and hadn't had a meal ready. He'd grabbed her so hard, she'd cried out in pain.

'It's time for you to move into my bed,' he snarled. 'I'm over this.'

'What?' Her eyes had been wide as he'd advanced on her.

'You bloody heard me. I've supported you and those little bastards for two years. And what do I get? Not a word of thanks from your bloody perfect brother, or one friggin' dollar. And what do I get from you, you frigid bitch?'

'I am *not* your partner, Jock. I share a house with you, and moving here was the biggest mistake I ever made.'

He shoved her so hard that she hit the wall and lost her balance, sliding down to the floor. As he moved towards her she cowered, his large frame looming over her as he grabbed her wrists and roughly pulled her to her feet.

'I'm going to the pub. You think about what I said.' He stormed out and slammed the door of the ramshackle house behind him.

She sobbed so much she'd found it hard to talk to Braden on the phone. Her words were jumbled, but she'd finally got it out. 'Bray? Can I come home, please? To stay? I want to come home. I have to come home.'

Locking herself in her bedroom she avoided Jock before he left for work the next morning. Braden and Kent had arrived in the afternoon. She hadn't seen or heard from Jock Evans since, and she didn't want to.

Chapter 11

Kilcoy Station – Sophie

Now, after three weeks in town, Sophie was finally going home. Just before she turned onto the last road that led to *Kilcoy Station*, a cloud of dust warned of an approaching vehicle. Braden and Callie and the boys passed her yellow Camry wagon with a toot of the horn. Callie waved madly and the boys grinned as they flashed past on their way to town. Sophie had left the Camry at *Kilcoy Station* when she headed up north with Jock. Braden had had it serviced a couple of times, and Callie had been driving it since she'd arrived to look after the boys.

Sophie knew she might as well have stayed in town and come out later after the billy cart races were over, but she probably would have been pressed for time, working at the pub tonight. She dumped her two bags in the breezeway and used her key to open the side of the house that hadn't been used since Julia's death.

She might as well get straight into it. Braden had tentatively agreed for her to live on this side. If there was too much to do to make it habitable, he would have to find someone else to work here as the cook, although if Sophie was honest, she was looking forward to getting back to what she loved doing. It had been a long time since she'd cooked.

During her sleepless periods throughout the night, she had come to the decision that from today, no one was going to tell her what to do. She had made poor choices twice over the past few years, and she knew why. If she'd been stronger, she wouldn't have gotten to the stage she had with Jock, and she wouldn't be feeling so depressed by last night's dream about Kent.

The door from the breezeway opened with a creak, and a blast of stale cool air greeted Sophie. Coming in here was going to be hard and she was pleased she was alone. She suspected Braden hadn't been in here since he'd locked this side of the house off two years ago.

Sophie wasn't sure what to expect; she'd lived out here with Braden and Julia when they were first married, and she knew going into this part of the house full of memories of Julia was going to be hard.

It had to be done.

She suspected there *would* be a fair bit to do before she even had a room ready to sleep in. A strange feeling overcame her and she held onto the doorknob tightly, reluctant to go any further. But she took a deep breath and forced herself to walk down the hall. She'd choose one of the guest rooms—not as many memories there—air it out, get some linen from her stuff she'd brought back from the north, make the bed and come here after her shift at the pub tonight. It would be a late night because the pub would be busy after the billy cart derby this afternoon. She'd brought her stuff that she'd taken from the house at Innot Springs. It had almost filled the small cargo hold in Kent's plane. There had been some stuff that she'd had to leave behind, but it wasn't important to her. Jock was welcome to it.

Sophie walked slowly down the hall, past Braden and Julia's bedroom, and the nursery where Petie's cot was still made up, a Disney mobile hanging motionless in the stale air.

Her eyes pricked as she paused in the doorway, and looked at the drawings that Julia had stencilled onto the wall before Rory was born. She had been so excited when their first child arrived.

'Oh, Julia.' Sophie sniffed as a tear spilled over. 'What a loss. What a waste.'

Julia had been like a big sister to her, and had been one of the few people—if not the only one— who had truly loved Sophie with no judgment, no criticism.

Julia had been there when she had found out what Kent had done. Julia had been the only one who knew. She had taught Sophie to be strong, and Sophie had used that same strength to put her grief aside and be strong for Braden after the accident.

Brushing the tears away, Sophie closed the door and walked down the dusty wooden-floored hall to the guest bedroom.

An hour later her new room was clean and fresh, the bed made up and the small ensuite wiped over. Her clothes were in the wardrobe, her treasured possessions on the shelves and her teddy bear on the chair next to the bed. Kent had won the purple teddy for her—a Tambo Teddy—at the Charleville show when they were in year twelve.

When they broke up, she couldn't bear to part with it, and Teddy had travelled with her. She'd shoved it in the bottom of a bag when Braden and Kent had picked her up so Kent didn't see it.

Her stomach grumbled and she looked at her watch. It was almost twelve. Sophie crossed to the wardrobe and took out her black skirt and white shirt for her shift at the pub, placing them into a plastic bag to take with her. She'd head to town now so she didn't miss the billy cart derby.

She'd make sure that Braden came in here tomorrow. It would be difficult for him but she'd be there for him. It wasn't fair to expect Callie to be involved. If Braden reneged, her brother would blow his chances of having her out here as the cook for the station staff.

They both needed closure. If Braden's relationship with Callie was to have any chance of succeeding, he had to let go of these physical reminders of the past. Memories would have to be enough.

With a determined head shake, Sophie backed out of the foyer and pulled the door shut behind her. She'd go to the billy cart derby and grab a late lunch there. She looked across at her car and pulled out her phone.

Braden picked up straight away.

'Bray it's me. Can I borrow one of the farm utes to come into town? I don't fancy driving home after the pub tonight in my car. Too many roos and emus about.'

'Home?' She could hear the satisfaction in his tone.

'Yes, home,' she said briskly. 'I've sorted out one of the guest rooms in your old wing.'

Silence.

'And I have a task for both of us,' she said. 'The rest of the rooms need sorting. It's time, Braden.'

'I know.'

'Can you get Callie to take the boys somewhere and you and I will get into it?'

'Not tomorrow. I've got a lot on at the rodeo.'

'Fair enough. But promise we'll get to it in the next few days?'

'Yes. I promise. And you don't have to ask about a ute. The keys are still hanging on the hook near the freezers in the breezeway.'

'Has the derby started?'

'Another hour. Rory went really well in the practice run. Try and get in here for the race.'

'I will. I'm leaving now.'

Sophie didn't look back as she drove one of the farm utes out and headed to town.

Chapter 12

Sophie's eyes widened as she searched for a parking spot around the corner from the pub. Normally quiet, Augathella was packed with cars, familiar and unfamiliar, all obviously in town for the billy cart races. The word about the good prizes on offer must have spread, and there were even a couple of cars with New South Wales number plates taking up some of the parks. Augathella hadn't been this busy for a long time.

Sophie locked her car and walked around the corner. Families lined both sides of the wide street, the smell of coffee and burgers came from the pub, and at least ten people said hello to her as she walked through the crowd looking for Braden, Callie, and the boys. She'd promised Rory and Nigel she would come and watch this afternoon. They'd been excited because they had helped Braden build a cart over the past few weeks.; it was good to see him taking such an interest in the boys now. She glanced at her watch; the nine years and under race was the first, and the races began at one o'clock. She had about half an hour to find them. The mood of the crowd was buoyant and she couldn't help smiling.

'Aunty Sophie. There's Aunty Sophie.' An excited squeal rang out above the noise of the crowd. Callie was holding Petie halfway up the hill.

Sophie waved to them and made her way through the crowd lining the footpath. A familiar voice made her pause as she almost reached Callie and Petie.

'You're full of it, love.' Old Reg, a well-known bushie from one of the outlying properties, his voice as distinctive as a saw cutting a rough piece of bloodwood wagged his finger at a young woman Sophie didn't recognise. 'I've never heard such a load of tripe in all my life.'

The woman grinned up at him and shook her head. 'Nope. I'm right. You can check.'

Sophie watched the exchange with interest. Reg was a true bushie; his face sported a long straggling grey beard, and an old tattered Akubra with more holes than brim sat on his head.

'And where, pray tell, would you suggest I check that ridiculous information?' Despite his appearance and his strange voice, Reg's words were always cultured.

'Google? The library?' The young woman's eyes danced with merriment.

"I still think you're pulling my leg.' Reg chuckled, and Sophie could tell he was enjoying the exchange. He doffed his battered hat and grinned at the woman. 'I will at that. The library it will be, first thing on Tuesday morning!' Reg turned and walked into the pub where Sophie knew he would spend the rest of the day. He'd been a regular there for as long as she could remember. He and a couple of other old locals would sit outside with a beer for the whole afternoon and watch the world go by.

The young woman turned with a wide smile and almost bumped into Sophie. 'Whoops, look out, Chilli,' she said apologetically.

For the first time, Sophie noticed the woman was holding a lead. A beautiful golden retriever looked up at Sophie as much as to say, 'Get me out of here.'

Please?

Sophie crouched down and smoothed her hands over the soft fur. 'Aren't you a beauty?'

The young woman replied. 'She is.'

'What's her name?'

'Chilli Girl, but I call her Chilli.''

'Hello, Chilli.'

The dog let out a satisfied groan as Sophie tickled her ears.

'She loves that.'

Sophie smiled at the dog's owner as she stood back up; she didn't recognise her. 'Are you visiting Augathella for Easter?'

'No, I've come here for work.' She held out her hand. 'I'm Amelia Foley.'

Sophie shook it. 'Welcome to Augathella. I'm Sophie Cartwright.'

'Cartwright? Are you Braden Cartwright's wife?'

Sophie chuckled. 'No, I'm his sister. You know Braden?'

'I haven't met him yet, but he interviewed me on the phone.'

Sophie's curiosity was piqued. 'Interviewed you?'

'Yes, I'm starting work at his station.'

Sophie stared and a strange feeling settled in the pit of her stomach. Maybe Braden had got sick of her stuffing around in town, avoiding going home.

'As the cook?' she asked.

'Heck, no!' Amelia shook her head. 'I'd poison anyone who was unlucky enough to eat what I cook. I have trouble opening a tin of baked beans, but I think it's because that's the last thing a person should have for a meal, don't you? I'm starting work as a ringer, but I prefer to be called a jillaroo. That has a much nicer ring to it, don't you think?'

Sophie nodded, as she tried to keep up with the conversation. 'I've never thought about it, but I suppose it does. So you're the one moving into the donga accommodation near the house?'

'Yes, that's me. But I'm on holiday until Tuesday. I'm meeting Mr Cartwright out there then. I heard there was an Easter festival in Augathella so I decided to come and suss out the town. I'm staying at the showground in my Landcruiser.'

'With your dog?'

'Yes, Chilli's a sweetie. Really well behaved. Loves people and she doesn't bark unless someone threatens me. Where I go, she goes. Dogs are wonderful companions, don't you think? No wonder they call them man's best friend. But they could say woman's best friend too. So many of those phrases that "they" come up with are sexist, don't you think?'

Sophie felt like she'd been hit with a volley of words, but she smiled. Amelia had a sweet personality, and she could see how she had become involved in a conversation with old Reg.

'Braden's here somewhere. The kids are going in the race. Does he know you have Chilli?'

'Oh yes, I checked I could bring a dog before I accepted the position. I have my own portable fence. Chilli will be fine and I won't let her go inside the donga. I assume it has a porch of sorts?'

'It does.' Sophie nodded. Curiosity took over. 'I'm moving back out there, to help Braden out, so I'll be cooking your meals. Tell me about yourself, Amelia. Where are you from?'

The more Amelia spoke, the less Sophie could imagine her working with the cattle on *Kilcoy Station*. Braden was in for a shock; he would have assumed a ringer would bring a working dog, not a golden Labrador.

And one with its own portable fence.

She grinned.

Amelia tilted her head to the side. 'I should have known you weren't Mrs Cartwright. I knew I'd heard your name. You won the date with the hot cowboy singer at the concert last night. So lucky.' She put her hand to her chest and fluttered her eyelids. 'I bought ten dollars' worth of tickets. A girl can always hope.'

Sophie drew in a deep breath and tried not to let it out in the sigh that threatened. She'd tried to forget about that, but Craig Wilson had caught up with her just before she and Kim had got on the bus to go back to town. He'd pressed a voucher into her hand.

'Here's your prize, Soph. There are a few noses out of joint that you won it.' To her horror, Craig had winked at her. 'Might be just what you need to bring you both to your senses, girl.'

She'd tried to hand it back to him. 'I don't think so, Craig. Give it to someone else.'

'No way. You won it fair and square.'

'No, I didn't. I didn't even buy a ticket.'

'Well, someone was looking after you. Enjoy your date.' With another grin, he'd turned and left her standing there holding the prize she didn't want. Sophie had shoved the voucher into her bag and tried to forget about it.

She let her breath out and looked at Amelia. 'Not lucky. Kent's just Kent to me. He's our neighbour. Not a hot cowboy singer. I tried to give the prize away, but apparently, I can't.'

Amelia straightened up and pointed up the hill. 'Look, they're lining up for the first race.'

'I'd better go. My nephews want me to see their rainbow billy cart. Do you want to come with me and meet Braden?'

'Sure.'

Amelia shortened Chilli's lead and walked beside Sophie as she walked up the hill to where Callie and Petie were waiting.

She lowered her voice and spoke quickly before they reached them.

'Amelia, just so you know. Braden is a widower, and Callie up here is his new partner. Just so you don't make the wrong assumption.'

'Thank you. Appreciate that. I'm always putting my foot in it. It drives my mother crazy. She tells me I should keep my mouth shut and think before I speak. You know she even wanted to send me to a finishing school in Switzerland to learn that sort of thing.'

Sophie stared. 'And did you?'

A finishing school graduate working as a ringer! Hell's bells, Braden. What have you hired? she wondered.

'No, I left home and worked on my first cattle station instead.'

Petie ran across to Sophie and hugged her legs. 'Aunty Soph, it's so exciting. Are you going to watch my big brother win the race?'

Sophie and Callie exchanged a smile.

'I hope so, Petie,' Sophie said. 'Callie, this is Amelia. She's coming out to work at *Kilcoy*. I'll leave her here with you, while I run up and see Rory and wish him luck.' She held Callie's eyes. 'And Petie, this is Chilli Girl. Give her a pat.'

Chapter 13

Kent

The Billy Cart Race

Kent crouched down behind the billy cart as Braden checked the front wheels were straight and tight. Nigel leaned over behind him and Kent grinned as the little boy tapped on Rory's helmet.

'Is your chin strap tight enough, Rory?' Nigel said loudly.

'It is. There's no need to yell.' Rory pushed his little brother's hand away.

Kent stood up and took Nigel's hand. 'Come on, mate. We have to go back behind the line so they can get ready to start the race. Your dad can stay there. You boys sure did a good job painting that billy cart.'

'Aunty Soph!' Nigel let go of his hand and took off.

Kent's attention honed in on the lithe figure in loose grey pants and a sleeveless shirt that clung to her body, her long brown hair loose on her shoulders. His stomach sank. He wasn't ready to face Sophie yet. He didn't care that she'd said he could sing well; it was calling him a fraud that had hurt, and then bloody Craig had drawn her name out and she'd won that stupid raffle Craig had created to raise funds for the local RFS.

I'm not a rock star, I'm a cattleman.

He saw the instant that Sophie noticed him standing there. She stopped walking up the hill and waited for Nigel to run to her.

Stuff it. He wasn't going to let her treat him rudely. Kent sauntered over and stood behind Nigel who was talking at nineteen to the dozen.

'Dad's told Rory *eggxactly* what to do. And I reckon he's going to win.' Nigel was jumping about, his words tumbling over one another. 'Did you see his helmet? Dad's going to buy me one for my new bike when I get it.'

'The cart looks pretty good. Love the paint job,' Sophie said. She looked up and her eyes snagged Kent's. No matter what had passed between them, no matter what he was supposed to have done, and no matter how rudely she treated him, Kent was damned if he could stop that bloody flutter in his belly every time he was with Sophie.

It was because they'd once been a couple.

That's all it is.

His body hadn't caught up with his heart yet. He didn't even particularly like her anymore. Her soft and happy personality had hardened; she wasn't the sweet girl he'd once fallen in love with.

But still, that was no reason for him to be rude back to her. Plus, he knew it really annoyed her when he spoke to her as though they were still mates.

'Morning, Sophie,' he said brightly. 'Ready for the action?'

Her lips tightened as she looked at him, and her eyes were hooded. 'Yes. It should be a fun day.'

'I hear you're coming back out to work at the station.'

'Perhaps.'

He stared at her. 'Braden told me you're cooking for the stockmen.'

'I might be.' She shrugged.

'I thought you'd agreed.'

'I said I *might* be. I won't be staying around so it depends what Braden needs and how long he needs me for.'

'Where are you going?' For the life of him, he couldn't hold back the question.

Another casual shrug. 'Don't know yet, but like I said I won't be staying here long.'

Before he could answer, Sophie gave him a dismissive glance and took Nigel's hand. 'Come on, Nigel, we've got to be down near the finish line when Rory comes down the hill.'

Kent refused to let Sophie's rudeness bother him and he turned to watch Rory as Braden leaned over and gave him some last-minute advice as the rainbow-painted billy cart sat on the ramp. On the other side of Annie Street outside the Evans' house, he could see Callie sitting in the shade with Petie on her lap. Fallon Malone and Jon Ingram were with her. They had a good vantage point about halfway down the track. Sending a swift look Sophie's way he checked she wasn't going over to them, and when he saw she was heading to the finish line across Main Street, he hurried over the row of tyres dividing the two lanes.

'Hey, Kent.' Jon held out his hand and shook it. 'I haven't seen you around for a couple of weeks.'

'Work's been full-on, mate. I know you guys are busy over at *Kilcoy Station* too.'

'We sure are. New staff ready to get sorted, and cattle to move. '

'Hi, Callie.' He smiled at Braden's partner and then turned to Fallon. 'You're looking well, Fallon.'

'Thank you, Kent. Now the morning sickness has passed, I'm feeling good. I'm ready to go back to work, but Jon talked me out of it.'

'Make the most of it. I hope you'll be back to work for the muster next year.'

'I will. My mum and dad are moving out to Augathella to live in Uncle George's house for a few months after the baby arrives.'

She was interrupted by Craig Wilson's booming voice as the PA came to life.

'Welcome everyone to the first heat of the Under Nines. All billy carts have passed the scrutineers' check and we're ready to go! Rory Cartwright and Evan Hudson are our first carts off the ramps. Just a reminder to everyone who is participating this afternoon in all age groups and opens, that no peddling, pushing, paddling or propulsion of any kind is permitted. We'll be watching! Now are you ready, boys?'

Kent grinned as Rory gave a thumbs up and Petie screamed out, 'Go Rory!' He turned to Fallon with a wide grin and said, 'That's my big brother.'

The race began and the screams around him cheered Rory on. At the bottom of the track, Sophie and Nigel were jumping and yelling and Kent forced himself to look away from her and focus on the end of the race. Her loose pants were cinched in by a wide black belt, and he thought how beautiful she was. As the two carts approached the finish line, the yells and screams got louder as Rory crossed the finish line a good metre ahead of his opposition. Braden ran down the hill and helped Rory out of the cart, sweeping him into a big bear hug.

Kent watched, feeling happy for the family. Life had certainly improved for them since Callie had come on the scene. Grief had etched wrinkles in Braden's face, but he smiled a lot more these days.

Braden ran up the hill with Rory on his back almost like the happy guy he'd been before Julia had died in that awful accident.

Kent stepped away and let them all make a fuss of Rory.

Jon and Fallon moved across to him.

'You going in the rodeo tomorrow, mate?' Jon asked.

'I'd like to,' Kent said. 'Depends on whether the cattle truck comes early enough. I've got some new steers coming. You going?'

'Wouldn't miss it. I'm one of the clowns.'

'Way to go. I forgot you did that when you were here before.'

'Bullride and bareback for you?'

'I've entered, but it depends on the truck.'

'You got all-round cowboy when I was here a couple of years ago from memory? I've never seen anyone ride like that. Either before or since.'

Kent nodded. 'Two years ago.' It had been the month after Julia's accident, and a few weeks after Sophie had broken up with him. He hadn't cared what risks he'd taken that year and had cleaned up on most of the events.

'Jeez, time flies,' Jon said.

'It does. Anyway, I've gotta go. Might see you there tomorrow.' Kent turned quickly and headed towards his truck. Sophie and Nigel were coming up the hill, and he didn't want to talk to her again.

It bloody hurt too much.

Chapter 14

Kent

Kent glanced at the clock on the kitchen wall and grabbed his Akubra and keys. He'd have to get a move on if he wanted to get his entry in for the steer riding. He'd had no intention of going to the rodeo; he had enough to do out on the station with the new steers arriving. The truck had arrived early, and he needed something to get his mind off Sophie Cartwright.

Work wasn't enough. He'd been on a high on stage on Thursday night but had come down with a thud after his words with Sophie at the billy cart derby yesterday. He'd convinced himself that he was over her, but since she'd come back to the district he couldn't get her out of his head.

Even though every interaction had been unpleasant, he didn't want to care about her anymore.

His head told him one thing, but every day his heart told him different. The day they flew up to that property at Innot Springs and collected her had been one of the happiest in his life. It seemed as if she had finally woken up to herself, and come home. Braden had silently pointed out the bruises on her wrists and if Jock Evans had appeared, he would have thumped him.

Self-disgust filled Kent. Even after she'd dumped him for that no-hoper and lived with Jock while they looked after Braden's boys, he should have known that Sophie didn't give two hoots for him. There was no way he'd try to rekindle their relationship.

Over and over he told himself, she wasn't to be trusted, but nothing worked. He'd even tried to get interested in Jennifer, but that was a disaster.

Sophie filled every waking thought. Maybe he needed to go and see someone. Perhaps he needed to call his mum and have her talk some sense into him.

As he pulled the back screen door shut, his mobile buzzed in his shirt pocket. A wry grin tilted his lips as he looked at his mother's face on Facetime call.

'Onya, Mum,' he thought. Not the first time he thought his mother had some sort of second sense where he was involved.

'Mum, hey there!'

'Hello, darling. How are you?'

'I'm great,' Kent lied. 'Just heading out to the rodeo.'

'I thought you might be.'

'Where are you and Dad?'

'We've just cruised into a place called Pioneer Bay in the Whitsundays. We're waiting our turn to get the launch to the town. Shopping, lunch and a swim in a huge lagoon pool. It looks divine from the photos.'

'How's Dad? Is he going okay?'

The joy in his mother's voice lessened a little bit. 'He's good. He had to go back down to the cabin. He forgot his wallet. Still forgetful.'

'But nothing worse?'

Kent had been worried about his father in the last few months on the station and had willingly taken over the management when his father admitted it was getting a bit too much for him.

'No. He gets cross because I keep a close eye on him. But he is fine. He's actually learned how to relax. He's read his way through half the library on the ship.'

'Good to hear.'

'He said to ask you how much rain you've had out there. He'd been watching the floods in the north-west. Jacinta never knows when we talk to her.'

'No floods here, but enough rain to give us a heap of feed, and fat and shiny cattle. I had a truck come in with more steers this morning.'

'He'll be pleased. He's proud of you, Kent. Now you tell me, how are you really?'

'I told you, I'm good. Why?'

'I was talking to Shirley Rogers on the phone last night and she told me Sophie Cartwright's back in town.' With her usual bluntness, his mother cut straight to the chase. 'So how are you coping with that?'

Kent leaned against the wooden boards of the old farmhouse and stared out over the paddocks. 'You're a mind reader, you know, Mother dear. I was just thinking about a chat with you when you called.'

'I knew you wouldn't be coping. Have you seen her yet?'

Kent let a small sigh of relief escape. He wasn't sure if anyone else knew the circumstances of Sophie coming home, and he didn't want to lie to his mother.

'Yeah, a couple of times. And she was at the billy cart races yesterday. Rory won his age division.'

'Good on him. So has she gone back home to *Kilcoy Station*? Shirley said that no-good fella she left with isn't with her.'

'I think she's going back to Braden's to cook for the contractors soon.'

'Good. I hope you don't intend to let her go again.'

'Whoa there, Mum!' Kent's fingers held the phone tightly. 'Sophie left of her own accord with another guy if you remember. She made it quite clear she didn't want me, so there's no chance of anything starting up between us.'

'Even though you'd like that?'

'Gawd, Mum. Give me a break.'

'I know you, son, and I know she's the woman for you.'

'Shame Sophie didn't think that.'

'Like I said, don't you let her go again.'

'That's not what I wanted to hear. Anyway, I'm seeing someone.'

'Who?'

'A new woman at the school.'

He didn't want his mother to focus on Sophie too much, but he lowered his voice and said honestly. 'Okay, I want you to tell me how to stop thinking about Sophie.'

'Well, there you go! I rest my case. If you still love her, give it your best shot.'

Kent was quiet for a minute.

'Are you still there?' his mother asked. 'And who are you seeing anyway? Do you think it may work out? That might help.'

'Yes, I was just processing what you said. I've been out a couple of times with the new counsellor at the school.'

'Do I know her?'

'No. She's only here part-time.'

'Listen, love. I have to go. The boat's here and your father's waving to me. I'll call you tonight, okay? Love you. And Kent?'

'Yes, Mum?'

'Follow your heart.'

'Love you too, Mum. Give Dad a hug for me.'

Kent was thoughtful as he made his way to his ute. His mood swung from hope to anger.

Follow his heart? Or trust logic?

There was no doubt that Sophie had betrayed him. Could he get over that and try to win her heart again? He pushed his phone into his shirt pocket. Even though it was good to talk to Mum—she was always good for advice—his mood had deteriorated.

Chapter 15

Sophie

Sophie rolled over in bed and glanced at the bedside clock she'd put on the side table. She was surprised to see it was heading for noon. Last night at the pub had been huge, and it was after one by the time she got back to the station. The wind was whistling outside; the first cold winds of autumn had arrived. She'd had to pull up a second blanket in the early hours.

For the first time, Sophie began to think that working out at the station would be better than being in town. Locals and tourists alike had crowded the dining room and bistro last night and Sean in his wisdom—because he had a second chef and a kitchenhand for the weekend—had decided to open for takeaway as well. It was all right at the kitchen end of things but Sophie had been in the front of house by herself.

Bistro, dining room, and takeaway. She was sure she'd run all night.

Literally. Taking orders, delivering meals and clearing tables from six until eleven. She was pleased she'd worn her joggers. At ten o'clock she'd hurried into the kitchen and seen the pile of plates waiting to be washed at the sink.

'Sean, if you think I'm loading the dishwasher you're wrong. Get the kitchenhand to do it.'

'But—' Young Kelly Leary pulled a face. 'I'm going out for drinks with my friends tonight. I'm already late.'

Sophie stared at Sean.

He pulled a face. 'If you want to keep getting shifts here, you can stay until eleven, Kelly,' he said.

'Not fair,' she grumbled.

Sophie had headed back out to deliver the last of the desserts and by the sound of the banging in the kitchen, she knew there was one unhappy young girl in there. But it had been a busy night and good for the town.

Now she lay in bed watching the autumn sunlight play across the ceiling. A vague sense of contentment crept over her. This was home, and she wondered if maybe she could be happy here.

Maybe—if the cooking job worked out—there'd be no need to take off for the city.

She shook her head. No, after Easter, she'd ring Damon Dean and see if there was any chance of taking up that scholarship. It wasn't fair on Braden and Callie for her to hang around, and it was too difficult with Kent nearby. The two stations worked closely together. A perfect example was yesterday, asking her questions about her job there. It was almost as though he was part of *Kilcoy Station* wanting to know the ins and outs. She'd call Brisbane tomorrow, and then she would have a definite time frame for Braden for the station cooking.

She climbed out of bed, took a shower and slipped on a warm and comfortable tracksuit. Making herself coffee and toast in the kitchen on the other side of the house, she picked up the *Southwest* newspaper that was on the kitchen table. The swinging chair on the verandah was a perfect spot once she manoeuvred it into the sun and settled in. The longer she sat out there, the happier she felt.

A short while later her mobile chirped and Sophie jumped, surprised to see the newspaper on the floor. Disoriented, she rubbed her eyes and reached for her phone

'Sophie, It's Braden. Are you coming into town for the rodeo?'

Sophie was surprised. 'Are you already there?'

'Yeah, we came in early. I'm part of the committee these days. Are you coming in?'

'I wasn't going to. I was late home last night.'

'Yeah, I heard you come in. I waited up until I heard you.'

A warm feeling suffused Sophie. It had been a long time since anyone had worried about her safety.

Or was it happiness she felt?

'Why do you want to know?'

Exasperation filled her brother's voice 'Hang on. Nigel! Last warning or you'll be going home.'

In the background, Sophie could hear Nigel crying at full volume. She instinctively reached out her hand as though she was there to comfort him. When Nigel was in a paddy he was inconsolable. 'What's wrong with Nigel?'

'He forgot his cowboy hat and all the other kids have theirs. I was hoping I'd catch you and you might bring it in.' Braden's voice held a wheedling tone. 'Please, Soph?'

Sophie held back a sigh. There went her relaxing day. 'Alright. But for Nigel. Not for you, big bro. And you'll owe me.'

'You're a—holy hell, gotta go.'

'What's wrong?'

'Kent's come off.'

Sophie put her hand to her mouth as Braden stopped talking. He mustn't have ended the call because she could hear him huffing as he obviously ran. In the background, she could hear the noise of the crowd. Her blood chilled as a siren overlaid the noise.

'Braden? Are you there? Is Kent okay?'

But there was no reply.

One of the reasons Sophie hadn't been fussed about going to the Easter rodeo was because she hated rodeos. When she and Kent had been together, she'd reluctantly gone along with him. She'd mainly gone to make sure he was all right, and she hated every minute of watching him in the ring. The year before his dad had handed the management of the property over to him, Kent had followed the season in western Queensland. That's where he and Braden had first met Jon Ingram. Jon had been one of the clowns at the Winton rodeo when Kent had won the bull ride. They'd hit it off and at that rodeo, Sophie learned that their actual job title was "protection athlete".

She'd hated the bull riding—it was known as the most dangerous sport in the world, but Kent had laughed.

'Nah, Soph. *Jon* has the most dangerous job. I'm *on* the bull, but he throws himself in the path of an 800-kilogram beast to keep me safe.'

Sophie had put her hand to her mouth and then grimaced as the red gritty dust settled on her lips. 'I hate the whole lot. Why on earth would you do that, Jon?'

At the time Jon had shaken his head and she leaned forward. It was hard to hear him speak over the noise of the crowd.

'Kent has more chance of getting hurt than we do. That's why we do it. For the guy on the bull, they're not in control. They're on the back of a beast—a cranky beast with an unwanted human on its back. A beast that weighs about 800 kilos. It's not a fair match. When the bull flings the rider down, they can't do much about it, and there's a chance of it turning into a nasty wreck. That's where we come in.'

Sophie shook her head. 'Well, I think you're all mad. One day it's *not* going to have a good ending.'

Kent had slipped his arm around her waist. 'We know what we're doing, Soph. I'd never put myself into danger.'

'Well, you just remember that, Kent Mason. You say you'd never put yourself in danger but look at what you do!'

'It's total focus, sweetheart.'

'I worry about you, Kent. It's bad enough when you're doing cattle work, this is unnecessary.'

That conversation stayed with her now as she shed her tracksuit, quickly pulled on jeans and a long-sleeved T-shirt, dragged her hair back and went looking for Nigel's hat.

Please, don't let today be that day. Ten minutes later, she was in the farm ute speeding towards Augathella.

Chapter 16

Sophie

Sickness roiled in Sophie's stomach as she turned onto Elmes Street where the rodeo grounds were. No matter what had happened or what Kent had done, she didn't wish him any harm. All the way to town as she bumped over the corrugations— she drove way too fast—she'd thought of the injuries she'd heard about at rodeos.

As she pulled up at the end of a long line of cars, an ambulance drove slowly from the ground and turned towards the main road.

No lights, no sirens.

The crowd was silent and panic built in her chest. That didn't look good.

As the ambulance passed the ute, Sophie caught sight of the sombre faces of two paramedics sitting in the front.

She grabbed Nigel's hat and her purse, slammed the door shut and ran towards the entrance. Once she'd paid her entry fee to a man she didn't recognise, she hurried through the crowd looking for Braden and Callie.

Finally, she spotted Braden with Jon—in full clown colours—at the chute where the broncos and bulls ran out. Trying to stay calm, she ran over to her brother, and not focusing on that last unpleasant conversation she'd had with Kent.

She had been a bitch, and it had been unnecessary.

What if he was . . .

No, he couldn't be. Braden and Jon were talking quietly together but looking calm. Even though Kent had let her down and broken her heart, she didn't want him to be hurt.

As she drew closer the crowd erupted in a roar as the gate to the ring opened. More cheers went up as two clowns ran into the ring and started a mock fight. They turned as the chute opened and half a dozen kids ran out holding ropes.

The noise of the crowd and the mood reassured Sophie a little but she still grabbed Braden's arm when she reached them. The smell of frying steak and onions reached her from the Lions' van, and she fought the nausea that rose.

'It's not bad, is it? If it was bad, they'd be quiet and going home, wouldn't they, Braden?'

'Is what bad?' Braden turned to her.

'Kent?' She swallowed. 'The ambulance?'

'No. He's fine, but they had to take him to Charleville.'

'If he's fine why would they take him to Charleville?

113

'You know we don't have X-ray facilities here. Kent's fine. Look here comes Rory.'

Sophie followed Braden's gaze to the ring and she couldn't believe what she was seeing.

'For God's sake, Braden? Are you mad? Letting Rory go out there?'

Braden stared at her, his face a picture. 'What's wrong now?'

Jon glanced her way and then jumped lithely over the rail and ran into the ring.

'Kent's just been taken to hospital and you're encouraging your son to participate in this awful sport?' Sophie's voice rose in pitch. 'How irresponsible are you?'

Braden put his hands on her shoulders, but she shook them off. 'Calm down, Soph. It's only dummy roping.'

'I don't care what it is. It introduces him to the sport. I suppose that's why Nigel wanted his hat.' She shoved the hat at Braden. 'Is he going in it too?'

'He is. And there's nothing wrong with it. They're country kids, Sophie. You of all people should know that. I remember you going in the dummy roping when you were a kid.'

She nodded, embarrassed by her attack on her brother. 'Yes, I'm sorry. You're their father. I was out of line.'

Braden put his arm around her shoulder. 'Don't worry. I know you would have been worried about Kent, but he's okay, so calm down. The other ambulance is on the way so we've brought the dummy roping event forward.'

'What's wrong with him exactly?'

'Busted arm and a nasty egg on his head where he hit the ground. Jon managed to distract the bull and Kent rolled over and got up by himself.'

'That's a relief. I was worried when you dropped out of the call.'

'I'm pleased to hear that. Shows you have a bit of kindness left in you.'

'What's that supposed to mean?' She put her hands on her hips 'If you don't want me around, I can soon head out.'

'Sophie, calm down. You're so bloody sensitive these days. I just meant that I've noticed how you and Kent dance around each other now. I was simply pleased to see that you were worried about him. I didn't mean anything by it and I wasn't having a go at you.'

'Of course I was worried. I'd worry about anyone. You know how much I hate rodeos.'

'You didn't always. After we watch Rory, we'll go grab a cold drink. There's something I want to ask you.'

She raised her eyebrows but smiled, trying to be a bit nicer. 'Hey, you owe me, brother. I brought the hat to town.'

'Good to see you smile, Soph. And you know, it's really good to have you back at home.'

Sophie shrugged. 'For a while. Where's Callie?'

Braden pointed to the grandstand. 'In the middle on the left with Petie. He wanted to go in it too, but he doesn't make the age cut.'

Before she knew it, Sophie was standing on the bottom rail of the fence cheering Rory on, as the local kids took turns to rope the dummy bull—a plastic head on a light metal frame on wheels.

She rolled her eyes as Rory got the rope around its head three times in a row, and took out first place. 'No stopping him now. I guess he's your son.'

Braden stood straight and grinned, pride evident in his expression as Rory ran over. 'Sure is.'

'What favour did you want to ask me? Spill, and then I'll go and get us all a cold drink and meet you in the grandstand.'

'I forgot I had a truck coming early tomorrow.'

'And, the favour is?' She knew what was coming.

'Can you go to Charleville and pick Kent up in the morning? I told him I'd get him, but I forgot about the cattle truck.'

'What about Jacinta?

'She's working at the races.'

'Oh.'

'You can take the good four-wheel-drive tomorrow,' Braden said.

'Well, thank you for that, but *if* I go, I'll take Gladys.'

'Come on, Soph, it's the least you can do.'

'What's that supposed to mean?'

'Sheesh. Don't be so bloody touchy. Kent flew me up to get you with absolutely no hesitation.'

Sophie lowered her eyes, her voice quiet as she realised she was being really hard to get on with. She had to figure out why she was in such a contrary mood. 'Alright. I'll go and get him.'

'Good girl. He's going to ring me when he's ready. I'll send you a message if I'm out with the truck.' Braden slung his arm around her shoulders as they walked over to the grandstand.

'And we need to sit down and have more of a chat too,' he added.

'What another one?'

'I want to know what happened with Jock.'

'Uh uh.' Sophie shook her head.

'I saw the bruises, Soph. I can guess what happened and I think you need to report it.'

'No, it's in the past now.'

'Maybe it is. But what if he does it again to someone else? Or worse? Or did he do worse to you?'

'No. He only had to do it once. And I knew I was out of there. I rang you as soon as he left.'

'So will you at least get it on record that he hurt you? Or threatened you?'

'I'll think about it.'

Chapter 17

Kent - Charleville Hospital

Kent cursed himself as he lay in the back of the ambulance. He should have known better than to ride that damn bull. He'd given in and let his mood govern his actions.

His head was fuzzy and random thoughts flittered through. He closed his eyes and opened them with a jump.

Can't go to sleep. Cattle to move.

Kent opened his eyes and focused on the roof of the vehicle above him, but it was too hard to focus. He closed his eyes again and concentrated on what he had to do at the station.

Bloody stupid thing to do, coming off that damn bull. His mind hadn't been in the ring, and when he'd come off, he should have rolled but he'd put his hand out to break his fall.

And broken his arm, or his wrist or whatever the X-ray was going to show. All he knew was it was hurting like a bastard, even with the pain relief the paramedics had administered.

The only good thing about it was that Sophie hadn't been there to see him come off. She would have taken great delight in telling him how stupid he was.

And I am, he thought.

Sophie. Images of her stayed in his thoughts. Images from years gone by.

Her beautiful green eyes filled with love as she'd looked up at him as they lay by the creek the first time they'd made love.

That thought *hurt*. He filed it away where it lived in his heart. What had he done that made her stop loving him? Because she *had* loved him. They had been so happy, and then almost overnight, the closeness went and she's taken up with that loser.

Maybe it was because bad boys held an attraction. Maybe he hadn't paid enough attention, and worked too hard, but Dad had been winding down and he'd been spending a lot of time out on the station. In the early days of their relationship, Sophie had loved spending time with Mum, but suddenly she'd stopped coming to *Lara Waters*.

His eyes blurred again.

Forget Sophie.

Focus on work.

After the recent rains, he had a lot to do at the station. At least the new steers had arrived and were okay for a while in the paddock he'd put them in. He was going to have to swallow his pride and ask for help, or maybe he could hire someone like Jon

Ingram?

Maybe Jon had some contacts? Kent's mood lifted a little. The only thing he wanted to make sure of was that his parents didn't feel as though they had to come home from their extended trip.

Anyway, he was pretty sure that while they were in Brisbane, Mum would be looking for somewhere for them to retire. She had a lot of family there, and as hard as it was going to be, it was close to medical care *if* Dad's health declined.

It sounded as though the progress of the disease had slowed, but the future looked bleak.

Kent nodded to himself as he lay there and a sharp ache gripped his head. He'd find someone to help for a couple of weeks, and he'd fly to Brisbane and meet Mum and Dad when the cruise ship docked.

##

Kent woke to a bright light shining in his eyes.

'Sorry, Kent. No sleeping until the doc checks you out.'

'Where are we?'

'Halfway to Charleville. Just stopped to take your obs.' Mitch, the local ambo, and a mate from school turned the small torch off. 'How are you feeling?'

'Like shit. But I'll live. I hope.' Kent managed a grin.

'Hope so.'

'You know you'll be admitted. Doc won't let you go home with a concussion, and I'd say you'll have a cast on that arm.'

'Hope not. Maybe I've just wrenched it.'

'You were going well until you came off. Paul and I had a good view from where the ambulance was parked.'

'You'll have to get back there so they can start it up again.'

'Nah, we had a second ambulance in town in case there was another one needed, so the events weren't held up.'

'I'd have been popular if that had happened.'

'Don't stress, mate. It's all good. You always did worry about others.'

'As long as it didn't ruin the day.'

'It didn't. Look you'll be back home before you know it. An X-ray and some attention to that arm, and you'll be as good as new.'

Kent saw the glance the paramedics exchanged and he knew they were concerned about him. 'I will be.'

Mitch glanced at Paul, the other paramedic. ' Do you know if the X-ray girl stayed or do we have to get a locum in again?'

'Larissa stayed. I'm taking her out for dinner tonight, so I'll have another trip back to town when we knock off.'

'Excellent,' Mitch said. 'Another city gal falls in love with the west.'

'Come on, let's get back on the road. Not far to go now, Kent.'

'You're not feeling nauseous?'

'No, just a bit fuzzy.'

'Good. Just stay awake.'

It was almost dark by the time Kent had been poked and prodded by Doc Henry, X-rayed by the sweet Larissa, and then plastered from wrist to elbow.

The doc was happy with his head injury but insisted on him staying for the night.

'How long will I have this on for?' Kent lifted his left arm as the nurse took his obs after he'd eaten a light dinner.

'Probably around six to eight weeks. It could take longer if the break isn't clean but apparently, yours was pretty basic. You'll need to wear your plaster cast until that broken bone heals.'

'Damn. I wonder if I can ride while it's on.'

'See what Doc Henry advises when he discharges you in the morning.'

'What time does he usually come in?'

She grinned. 'I can guarantee it will be early. He'll be keen to get to the races at Augathella.'

'Damn, I forgot about the races. I'm supposed to be helping there.' His smile was rueful. 'And yeah, the doc likes a flutter, and he always picks a winner. Knows his horses.'

The nurse smiled sympathetically as she clipped the board on the end of the bed. 'Sleep well.'

When she'd gone, Kent reached for his phone. Luckily it had survived the fall; he'd zipped it into his front shirt pocket. He pressed speed dial for Braden.

'Hang on, mate. I'll just go outside.'

Kent could hear voices, loud music and kids yelling. He waited for a minute.

'We're at the pub.'

'Yeah, I could tell. Lucky you. Have a beer for me.'

'How are you? Gonna live?' Braden asked.

'A bloody broken wrist and a mother of a headache. Should be right to go in the morning. Listen don't worry about getting me. I forgot the races were on. I'll sort a lift home from here. Doc Henry might even give me a lift.'

'Don't worry about travelling with Doc. I've sorted a lift for you. Gotta go, mate. See you when you get home. I'll organise someone to help you with those steers too.'

Before Kent could respond, Braden disconnected. Probably having a great time at the pub with all the families and friends who would be there. If he'd been more focused he could be there too, instead of lying alone in an old hospital room a hundred kilometres from home.

With a sigh, Kent lay back on the pillow and closed his eyes.

Chapter 18

Sophie

Sophie was up at the crack of dawn and headed for the kitchen.

Might as well get it over and done with. The sooner she got to Charleville, collected Kent and dropped him at *Lara Waters*, the sooner she could stop worrying about it. Being in a car with him for an hour was going to test her willpower. With a bit of luck, she could drop him at his ute in town and he could drive to *Lara Waters* from there.

You could drive with a cast on, couldn't you?

They'd never really talked about what had happened between them and she didn't want to start now. The thought of the two of them in a car together terrified her; she knew that was why she was so unsettled. Kent had tried, but she'd clammed up. To verbalise what had happened would reduce her to a blubbering mess, and she hadn't wanted him to see her like that.

Now, she didn't want to see him at all, and she didn't want to talk to him.

I don't.

Really.

She wanted to take her car this morning because she had the car audio system connected to her phone and they could have music on, to save the need for a conversation on the way back. She'd take it slow and watch out for kangaroos.

To her surprise, Braden was in the kitchen when she went across, and the smell of fresh-brewed coffee greeted her.

'Morning, brother. That smells good.'

'Mm.' The sound was closer to a grunt.

'Sore head, hey?'

'A bit.'

'I'm not surprised. I could hear you from the bistro last night. I take it Callie drove home?'

A nod.

'Late?'

Another nod.

'What time's the truck coming?'

'Soon.'

She watched as Braden poured a mug of coffee for her and passed it over. 'Ta.'

'Bistro was busy again last night.' Finally a whole sentence from her brother.

'Yeah. You'll be pleased to know I gave Sean my notice last night. I can't cook here and work nights there too.'

'Good.

'You want me to start Monday of next week?'

'Yes, please. And I've already put you on the books. No arguments.'

'Okay, and I'll pay board.'

'You won't.'

'I will.'

Braden pulled out a kitchen chair and sat down. Sophie crossed to the coffeemaker and filled her travel mug.

'Look, Braden. The contract workers pay board. I can't freeload off you,' she said as she pulled out a chair and sat opposite him.

'For Christ's sake, Sophie. You're family.'

She stared at him.

'And not only that, how much do I owe you for taking the boys for all those months? And I don't mean money. I mean, I *owe* you. We won't discuss it again. You're not paying board.'

Sophie shrugged.

The only noise was the hum of the fridge as they drank their coffee. Finally, Braden broke the tense silence.

'The contract ringers and the two new permanents arrive on the weekend. So it's good that you're here now.'

'I met one of the new staff in town at the billy cart derby the other day.' Sophie closed her eyes as she sipped the strong brew. Somehow it always tasted better when Braden made it. 'Did you end up meeting her? Amelia was her name.'

'No. I was busy with Rory. My little champion.' Braden's grin was wide. 'But she's coming out here tomorrow to check out her digs.'

Sophie frowned wondering whether to say anything about her dog but decided against it. It was none of her business. 'She seemed really nice. Likes a chat. She had old Reg lined up. They were having quite an intense talk.'

'He does like a chat.'

Sophie stood and took her mug to the sink. 'I'd better go.'

'He hasn't called yet,' Braden said.

'I don't want to be back late. Sean's got me working with Kelly this afternoon to show her how to set the tables.'

'It's not rocket science, is it?' Braden frowned. 'So you won't be at the races?'

'No.'

'Me either. We've had a big enough Easter, and I need to catch up on some work. I'm surprised you're not going. Couldn't you have swapped a shift? I thought you'd want to keep your winning streak going for Fashion of the Field.'

'I'm not really interested in it anymore. Most of my friends have moved away and . . .'

'And it's something you and Kent used to do together.'

'No. I wasn't going to say that.' Sophie glared at him. 'Just let it go, okay?'

'Okay, okay.' Braden put his hands up. 'Listen, change of subject. Do you want me to hire someone to help you with the clean-up and stuff down in the cookhouse?'

'No, I can handle that. I mean I'm only cooking for how many? Eight? Ten?'

'Yep. Ten.'

'I'll be fine.'

Sophie picked up her travel mug and headed for the door.

'Sophie? Have you got any days off this week?'

'Tomorrow and Wednesday. Sean's going to see how Kelly goes by herself. Why?'

'I thought we might get in and . . . get in and sort out . . . Julia's stuff.'

Sophie walked back to the table and put her hand on her brother's shoulder. 'Sounds like a plan.'

'Callie'll be in town at school both those days, and Petie will be at kindy and the other two at school.'

'I'm in.'

Braden cleared his throat and met her gaze squarely. 'I want to tell you first, Soph. I'm going to ask Callie to marry me. What do you think of that?'

'I think that's wonderful news. I've seen the way you look at her. I know you love her, and that's all that matters.'

'No one will ever replace Julia, but she's gone.' Braden's voice broke. 'I have to move on. And like you said, clearing out the house is the first step. It needs doing. It's past time.'

Sophie shook her head. 'I was too harsh with you. No, not past time. You needed time to grieve. If you're ready to do it now, it's time. I'll help. And if it gets too hard, we'll soldier on together.'

'Thanks. I'll go over and see Kent this afternoon, and get his big trailer. I thought we might get new furniture for the house too. Give it a real turnout.'

'Leave it a while and include Callie in that.'

'That's a good idea. But I have to wait until she agrees to marry me. I worry I'm rushing her and that she'll say no. She's never lived in the outback. She'd not had anything to do with cattle work, and I've got the boys.'

Sophie nudged Braden with her shoulder. 'Three boys she loves and is fantastic with, and you've no need to worry. I've seen the way she looks at you.'

'It's a big ask, Soph.'

'There's only one thing I'd worry about. How would you feel about having more kids? Does she want children?'

'We've never talked about it.'

'Well, my advice is, talk to her. Communicate. Most relationship problems come from lack of honesty.'

'Is that what happened with you and Kent?'

'That subject's closed, Braden. So leave it.'

'If you ever need to talk . . .'

'I know. I have a big brother with a soft heart and a good ear. I'll keep you in mind.'

'Okay. Don't forget to ask Kent about the trailer. If it's okay. Tell him I'll go over after lunch.'

'Speaking of which I'd better get going.' She turned to leave again, but Braden grabbed her hand. His fingers were rough and callused against hers. 'Soph? Be kind to Kent. He's a good man.'

She raised her eyebrows. 'Is he?'

'You know he is. I'd love to see you two get back together. For the life of me, I don't know why you ever broke up. And neither does Kent.'

'Well, that's not going to happen, Braden. You need to accept that and butt out. Once you get a permanent cook, I'll be leaving.' Sophie's temper began to fire and she strode out of the kitchen before she said something she'd regret. She and Braden had made their peace, and she wanted it to stay that way.

Kent? A good man?

Pah! She'd thought that once too.

She'd loved him with her heart and soul before he let her down.

Chapter 19

Kent

'Thanks, Doc. One more question. Can I drive with this thing on?' Kent nodded down at his plastered arm, now supported in a sling.

'In a day or two, as soon as the headache and dizziness have been gone for twenty-four hours,' the old doctor replied.

'It's all gone now.'

'So if it stays away, you can drive tomorrow. But don't overdo it, Kent. I know what you cattlemen are like. You think you're invincible.'

'We are. Almost.' Kent grinned. 'A favour? Are you going to the races in Augathella today?'

'Sure am. Want a tip?'

'No, I'm hoping for a lift.'

Doc shook his head. 'You don't need one. Your driver's waiting for you in the waiting room.'

'Great, Braden's a good mate.'

Doc looked at him curiously. 'Okay, if you have any more headache issues or blurred vision, you get straight to the clinic. Anyway, come and see me in two weeks, and I'll see how that arm's going.'

'Thanks, Doc. I'll take it easy.'

The old doc's wrinkled face split into a grin and he tapped his nose. 'And just for the record, *Spyzain's* a sure thing in race three.'

Kent grinned back. 'Got it.' The old doc was legendary with his horse knowledge.

Once the discharge papers were signed, Kent went into the bathroom and dressed in the clothes he'd been wearing yesterday. They took a bit of dusting down. He went to cup his hands under the tap and wash his face, but the damn cast held him up. The next few weeks were going to be bloody difficult.

Five minutes later he'd managed to wash his face and slick back his hair. He put his phone in his pocket and headed out to the waiting room.

There was no sign of anyone there, and he wondered if the doc had been mistaken. He pulled out his phone to call Braden, but he was interrupted by a voice behind him. A voice he knew very well.

'Kent.'

He turned slowly, putting his phone back in his pocket, as he tried to control the increase in his heart rate.

'Sophie? What are you doing here? Did Braden send you in?'

'I don't know what you mean by *in*, but yes, Braden asked me to come to Charleville and get you. He's got a cattle truck in this morning.' Sophie stood there, dressed in a pair of jeans and a long-sleeved close-fitting T-shirt. It struck Kent how much weight she'd lost; he hadn't noticed before. Then again, he tried not to look at her. It hurt too much.

He had to bite his tongue not to comment, and when he spoke his words were garbled. 'You drove all the way to here, I mean to Charleville to get *me*?'

Her voice was matter-of-fact, and he was pleased it didn't hold any of the angst of the other night. 'Well, you went much further to collect me when I needed to get home. I owed you.'

'Well, it's very kind of you. But you didn't need to pay me back. I could have found my own way home today.'

'That may be the case, but I'm here now, so you might as well come with me. Do you need to do anything before we go? My car's in the car park.'

'No. I'm right to go. Doc Henry signed me out.'

'Good. Come on then. I have to get back quickly because I'm working this afternoon.'

Sophie strode off and Kent watched as she headed down the corridor ahead of him. Halfway along, she stopped and turned.

Her face was closed as she waited for him to catch up.

'I'm sorry,' she said when he caught up to her near the lift. 'I didn't ask how you were feeling. Do you need a wheelchair?'

'No. I certainly don't. I've got a broken wrist, not a leg.' Kent knew his tone was curt. He hated being at a disadvantage. Even though his head was still a bit achy, the last thing he wanted was Sophie pushing him along in a wheelchair. 'And I'm feeling fine.'

Nothing more was said until they reached the car park. Kent's eyes widened in surprise. 'You've still got Gladys?'

Their eyes met over the top of the yellow Camry wagon and the look they exchanged held lots of memories.

'Yes. I left her at Braden's when I moved away.'

Moved away? Kent thought. More like *ran* away.

Sophie waited beside the door as he climbed into the passenger seat. When he was in, she closed the door for him, walked around and got in the driver's side.

Kent felt totally useless, his left arm in a sling. He reached down and did his seatbelt up. At least he could do that by himself.

Being in a confined space with Sophie for over an hour was going to be hard. It would be a great opportunity to ask her all the questions that he'd had for her when she dumped him so suddenly, but he didn't want to get her offside yet.

They were both quiet as she started the engine and reversed out of the hospital carpark. He put his head back and closed his eyes.

Damn, she still wore that same floral perfume. He hadn't noticed it until they got in the car. All he could think of was how he used to nuzzle his nose into the soft skin of her neck and inhale the fragrance.

'Is your head aching?' she asked softly.

'A little bit,' he replied honestly.

'I was going to play some music on the way back,' she said.

So you didn't have to talk to me, he thought.

'Would it bother you?' she asked.

'Possibly.'

He noticed her fingers tense on the steering wheel as she waited to turn left onto Sturt Street.

'Okay. I'll leave it off and I'll keep quiet. Go to sleep if you want,' she said.

'No, it's fine. We can chat.'

This time her fingers were white from gripping the wheel.

'You're probably better to rest.'

'No, I'm supposed to stay awake.' It was only a little white lie. 'We can catch up on each other's news.'

How prosaic that sounded.

Catch up on each other's news?

Here he was sitting in a car with the woman he had once loved so much.

If he was truthful, she was the woman he still loved, even though she had treated him so callously.

What he'd like to do was be honest and tell her how she'd broken his heart and find out once and for all why all of a sudden he hadn't been enough for her.

Why she'd left him for that no-hoper.

This was going to be a very long trip home to Augathella.

Chapter 20

Sophie

This was going to be the longest trip she'd ever driven back to Augathella. Her car had never seemed so small as it did this morning. As she reached down to put it into drive, she had to keep her fingers to the right so she didn't accidentally brush Kent's jeans.

Three years ago, in this same car—Kent had called it Gladys because he said it reminded him of his mother's Aunt Gladys; she always wore yellow. In those days they'd even held hands as she'd driven.

Sophie swallowed when he said they could catch up on each other's news. That was the last thing she wanted to do.

'Not much news to tell here,' she said crisply. 'I'm only home for a while to help Braden out, and then I'm off.'

Kent didn't answer and she searched for something else to say, something that didn't relate to them. Then again, there was no them.

That was in the past.

She scouted around for a safe topic. 'So how's cattle prices been here?' She finally came up with something away from the personal. 'I haven't had a chance to ask Braden.'

'Not bad. Not good.'

'Fair enough. I heard that the big muster went well.'

'Yes. It did.'

Sophie tried to focus on her driving. Once they would have chatted nonstop, their words tumbling over the other's.

'How are your parents?' As soon as she asked that she regretted it.

No. Too personal. Way too personal.

'Mum's good. Dad's not well.'

'I'm sorry to hear that.'

'He's been diagnosed with early-onset Alzheimer's.'

Sophie drew a quick breath as shock filtered through her. For the first time her words were genuine. 'Oh no, Kent, that's awful news. Braden didn't tell me.'

'Braden doesn't know. I haven't been able to talk about it. I guessed I thought if I didn't tell anyone, it mightn't be real.'

'How's your mum handling it?'

He turned to look at her, and she took her attention off the road briefly. Their eyes met and a warm feeling uncurled low in her stomach.

141

'You know Mum. She's always positive and sees the good side to everything. That's why she took Dad off on this three-month cruise. She said they would have a good time, and it would be something they could remember together.'

He clenched the fingers of his right hand until his fingers were white, but didn't say anything more.

Sophie cleared her throat. 'I loved your mum. You know that. And I loved your dad too. I mean I still do. I feel for her, it's an awful thing. Maybe he won't deteriorate too quickly.'

'Maybe not. We can only hope. Mum and Dad love you too, Sophie.'

Shit. She didn't want the conversation to get so personal. They were barely on the road to Augathella. There was still an hour to go.

Kent half-turned in the passenger seat and she saw his wince as he readjusted his sling.

'Have you had some painkillers today?'

'No. I didn't want them. I need to have a clear head.'

Sophie sensed his eyes on her and discomfort settled in her stomach as warmth moved up her neck.

'It's good to talk about it, Sophie. Maybe I'm overreacting. Maybe it won't be as bad as my imagination plays out at night.'

'Well, I'm here and I'm listening, so talk as much as you want.'

Strangely she meant it. It broke her heart to hear what Mr Mason was going through. Even though she called Kent's mum by her first name, she'd never felt right calling Mr Mason anything else. He had teased her about it and always joked with her.

'One day, I hope you'll be calling me Dad, Sophie,' he'd said the last night she'd had dinner at their house.

And then her world had fallen to pieces.

'I'm pleased you're listening. I'm pleased we're actually talking. It's been a long time. I miss those days, Soph. Mum and I were talking about you yesterday morning.'

'Oh.' Her voice was quiet.

'Yes, she'd heard you were home. She was full of all sorts of advice.'

'For me?' Sophie frowned.

'No. For me.'

Neither of them spoke for a while. Sophie wondered what Rhonda Mason would have advised Kent, although if she was honest she had a fair idea. She also knew that Rhonda wouldn't have known what Kent had done. She doubted if anyone else did either. It must have burned out quickly.

Hold that thought, she told herself. Remember what he did. She could feel sorry for the family, and what they were going through, but that didn't mean automatic forgiveness for Kent.

'Do you want to hear what she said?'

Sophie shook her head. 'No. Try to rest. We'll be in town soon.'

'I'd like to try and talk to you, Sophie.'

'We're talking.'

'No, I'd like to talk about us. Mum's advice was clear.'

'No, Kent. You and I don't have anything to talk about.'

'Will you just answer one question for me? One question, with an honest answer. It's time I moved on.'

Chapter 21

Kent

Kent stared ahead, not game to look across at Sophie. He wondered what she'd do if he pressed the issue. Knowing how strong-willed she was, he wouldn't be surprised if she even pulled up and put him out at the side of the road.

But while they were together in this small car, and he had her attention he was going to push. They'd never talked when she'd broken it off. He'd been hurt, and then when she moved in with Jock Evans, anger had taken over. He'd vowed never to trust another woman as long as he lived.

'All right, one question, but if I don't want to answer, I won't.' She stared straight ahead and focused on the straight road.

'Right. But I'd appreciate honesty. Mum told me to follow my heart on the phone yesterday, and I can't do that until I have closure.'

'Closure from what?'

'Closure from us.'

'There is no us.'

'No, there isn't, but there was for a long time.'

'So what's your question?'

145

Kent took a deep breath and tried not to frown when pain ran up his arm into his shoulder.

'Why did you stop loving me? Was it something I said? Something I did that you decided you didn't like? Did I outgrow you? Was I going too fast?'

'One question, you said. Which one do you want me to answer?' Her lips were set in a straight line, but he could see the tension in her shoulders and heard the quiver in her voice.

He moved in the seat, and his arm throbbed again. Tension filled his body as he thought. 'The main one, I guess.'

'The main one? Which one would that be?'

'For God's sake, Sophie, don't be so bloody close-minded. Listen to me. I'm trying to find out why you stopped loving me. Maybe I shouldn't have said anything. It's so bloody hard. I've tried to move on. It's been over two years now, and you know what, I can't. How can I try to love someone else when I don't know what's wrong with me? How can I trust someone else to love me, and keep loving me?'

He finally found the courage to look at her. Two spots of deep pink coloured her cheeks, and as she turned to him briefly her eyes flashed with anger.

'You poor thing! You thought you could get away with what you did, and sweet little Sophie would be there waiting for you.' Her words were bitter and Kent widened his eyes.

'Get away with what I did? What did I do?'

'Don't, Kent. Just don't. I've moved on. I've forgotten about it. I don't want to rehash it all. You hurt me so badly, I had no choice.'

'I hurt *you*? You're the one who broke it off and moved in with another man, not even a month after I'd planned to ask you to marry me. I even had the ring. And what did I get? A phone call telling me we were done. You didn't even have the guts to come and tell me why, face-to-face!'

'Because I knew if I looked at you and you said you were sorry, I'd probably forgive you and regret it for the rest of my life. I know everyone wanted us to get married. Your parents, Braden, the whole bloody town, but *you're* the one who ruined it so don't you dare blame me.'

Confusion filled Kent. He shook his head and the movement bloody hurt. 'I have no idea what you're talking about.'

'Don't make it worse with a lie. You're the one who brought it up. You can't take the truth? So drop it.'

Kent reached over and put his good hand on her arm. His stomach sank when she flinched and he moved his hand back quickly. 'Talk to me, Sophie, please. Tell me what you mean.'

'No. There's no point. I told you two years ago, Kent, that we were through. It's time you accepted it.'

'Did you do the same thing to Jock? Is it that you just can't commit, Sophie?' He regretted his words as soon as they came out.

'That is none of your business.' Her voice broke and he knew it had been a low blow.

'I'm sorry. That was out of line. Can't you see—'

Anger hummed through the silence in the small car. She reached forward and turned the music up so loud it thumped through his aching head

Kent put his head back and closed his eyes.

Well, that went well. Thanks for the advice, Mum.

Not another word was spoken until they reached the outskirts of Augathella.

'My ute's at the rodeo ground. Drop me off there.' He couldn't even come up with "please".

He didn't care what the doc said about not driving until tomorrow. If he ran off the road, who would care?

As he unlocked the door of his ute, Kent regretted that thought. A lot of people would, and he wouldn't do that to his parents.

From this moment on, he wasn't going to give Sophie Cartwright another thought.

Maybe he'd call Jennifer and see if she'd like to come out for a visit. He was going to go stir crazy sitting out there by himself, and not being able to work.

He didn't let himself think of the emotions that Sophie Cartwright had brought screaming back.

Chapter 22

Sophie - that evening

Sophie stared back as Kelly dropped the knives and forks she was holding and gestured angrily at the half-set table.

'So what's wrong with that? And why are you so shitty?' the young girl demanded.

'I'm not "shitty" as you put it,' Sophie replied coldly. 'Have you never set a table before? Or at least had a meal at a properly set table? This is the dining room and it's more upmarket than just collecting your cutlery and packets of salt and pepper at the bistro. That's why the prices are higher in the dining room. And *that's* why we make it look good.'

Kelly's voice was scornful. 'What? You pay more for a meal in here because someone arranges the cutlery on the table. What a bloody rip-off.'

Sophie tried not to grit her teeth and counted to ten under her breath. 'That's correct and you are going to be the someone who sets the table correctly.'

'Well, I'm the waitress, and I don't see why I have to be the one to set the tables too.'

Sophie rolled her eyes. 'So who's going to set them? Will we get Sean to come out of the kitchen and do it? Or maybe Hilly can leave the bar and come and do it instead?'

'Don't be smart-mouthed, and you are shitty. And you're only a waitress too!' Kelly's hands went to her hips.

'Only for two more nights, thank God,' Sophie retorted. 'So, pay attention and we'll get these tables done.' She moved across to the next table. 'Now watch me. Fork on the left. Spoon and knife on the right. Bread and butter plate to the left of the fork.'

'For God's sake, does it really matter? If they want to eat, they'll find their cutlery.'

Sophie's temper finally boiled over. 'Look, Kelly, if you don't listen and do what I show you you'll likely be out of a job.'

'I don't really care. I'm more interested in what's wrong with you. Did you have a fight with your boyfriend or something?'

'Not that it's any of your business, but I don't have a boyfriend. Now you watch me do this table and you do that one.'

As Sophie pointed to the round table beside Kelly, her thoughts weren't focused on the table setting.

151

Instead her thoughts were on, *"or something"* as the young waitress had said.

An hour ago, Sophie had pulled up beside Kent's ute in the car park at the rodeo grounds. She'd sat there tight-lipped as he got out without a word.

Guilt ripped through her as she drove across from Riverside into town. She'd pulled up at Meat Ant Park and walked across the soft grass and sat on one of the seats trying to calm down.

Leaving Kent to fend for himself had been the wrong thing to do, but she couldn't take any more. If she hadn't promised to help Braden tomorrow, and if she hadn't committed to cook until he found someone permanent, she would have packed Gladys and just left.

And where would you go? that little nagging voice asked her. The same little voice that had told her she was doing the wrong thing moving away with Jock. But she hadn't been thinking straight back then. All she'd thought of was the boys needed to be with their father. Jock had tried for a relationship, but by that time she'd known what he was after, and it wasn't her.

She wasn't good at making decisions, so she'd stay and help Braden until she got her thoughts in order and her emotions back in check.

On her way to the pub to start her shift, she called into the police station and asked them to put on record what Jock had done. It was time to stand up for herself. She'd been a fool to go with him, and for the life of her she didn't know why she had.

'So?' Kelly's voice made her jump.

Sophie blinked and looked around the dining room. The tables were all set and as far as she could see, everything was in the right place.

'Good. Looks good. Thank you.'

'You were off with the pixies, so I copied the one you did. Are you okay, Sophie? You look really unhappy.'

Sophie cleared her throat. 'Yes, I'm fine.' She forced herself to smile. 'Just a bit on my mind, but thanks for asking. Are you right to help Sean with the cold larder now? I'm going to take a short break. I have to make a quick phone call. Lunch rush won't start for half an hour.'

Kelly nodded and headed for the kitchen.

Sophie went out to the small yard at the back of the pub where caravans often pulled up. Six caravans and two campervans filled the space, but they were all locked up and there was no one in sight. The tourists would all be at the races. She pulled out her phone and walked along the grassy footpath as she waited for Braden to pick up the call.

'Hey Soph, did you get him home okay?'

'I got him back to town and dropped him at his ute.'

'God, he's a stubborn bugger. I hope he was okay to drive home.'

'He should be out at *Lara* by now. You're going over there, aren't you? Maybe you could give him a call and check he got home safely.'

'I'll go over in a while. I've got a pump to move first. How was he feeling this morning?'

'He was okay.'

'Are you?'

'Why?'

'You sound funny.'

Sophie stared along the street as she reached the corner. Old Reg was sitting at a table at the front of the pub. A schooner of beer sat in front of him and he lifted a hand and waved when he spotted her. Sophie managed a smile and stayed on the corner as she spoke to her brother.

'I'm all right. Probably should have driven him all the way, but we sort of had words.'

'Sort of.'

She stayed quiet.

'Okay, he's a big boy. I'll be a couple of hours yet. Amelia should be here by the time I get back to the house.'

'Amelia? I thought she was coming out tomorrow.'

'Changed her mind. And it suits because you and I have plans for tomorrow. I think she's going to move in early, so I might need you to cook a couple of meals before the weekend.'

'I can do that. And if I'm cooking I can do some for Kent and maybe drop them over.' Sophie surprised herself when that came out.

'That'd be neighbourly.'

'I have to get back to work. See you tonight. Say hello to Amelia and Chilli for me.'

'Chilli? Does she have a partner?'

'You'll see.'

'Okay, I'm sure I will. Listen, did you ask Kent about the trailer?'

'Sorry, I forgot. Gotta go.'

Reg had finished his beer and gone into the bar to get another one, so Sophie hurried along past the front of the pub to the door of the dining room. As she was about to step inside, a car pulled up and a dark-haired woman got out and hurried around to the footpath.

Sophie froze and stared as the woman opened the back door and unstrapped a toddler from a baby seat. Hitching a bag over one shoulder, she held the child with one arm. She must have sensed Sophie staring because she turned and looked over at her. Her lip curled and Sophie braced herself.

'Come back to town with your tail between your legs, have you, Sophie?' Ros Evans, Jock's sister stared at her with dislike.

Sophie lifted her chin and held her gaze. Ros had been a couple of years below her at high school. Sophie hadn't liked her then, and she liked her a lot less now. In fact, she could barely look at her after what had happened.

'Too good for my brother, were you? Poor Jock's heartbroken.'

The events of the morning: Kent's persistence in trying to rehash the past, Kelly's incompetency and whining, and now seeing her nemesis, tipped Sophie over the edge. Her temper flared and she took a step toward Ros.

Her voice was cold. 'Your brother's lucky not to be up on a charge. The police were insistent that I press charges.'

'Oh, you poor diddums.' The malice fair dripped off Ros's words. 'It was probably only what you deserved.'

Sophie's mouth dropped open. 'Are you serious! You think it's all right for a man to hit a woman?'

'Like I said, you probably deserved it.'

Sophie shook her head slowly. 'No woman deserves that, and no woman should have to put up with it. I feel very sorry for you with that attitude.'

'Now you're back in town, are you going to cosy up with Kent baby, again?' Ros leaned forward, a sneer on her face. For the first time, Sophie noticed the fine wrinkles around her mouth and her lank hair. Ros lifted the toddler onto her hip. 'Just one word of advice. You be careful there, honey. Good old Kent might be the golden-haired boy around town, but he doesn't take responsibility for his actions.'

Sophie looked at her in horror as Ros gestured to the toddler on her hip. 'Doesn't want to know about you, does he, little man?'

Cold seeped into her chest as she took in the little boy's dark hair and olive skin.

Just like Kent's.

Chapter 23

'Morning, Sophie.' Callie called as she herded the boys across to the garage. 'Sorry can't stop to chat. There's a staff meeting this morning. Coffee's on.'

'Hi everyone. Have a top day.' Sophie smiled as Petie ran over to her and wrapped his arms around her legs.

'You have a topsy day too, Aunty Sophie.'

She bent down and hugged him. 'I will have a topsy day, Petie, now hurry up and follow Callie. You don't want to be late for kindy.'

Callie waited for Petie to run across to her as the other two boys raced into the shed.

'I'm in the front today,' Nigel called out.

'No, it's my turn.' Rory's voice echoed from the garage.

Callie rolled her eyes and then her gaze held Sophie's. 'You okay?'

'A bit tired. I didn't sleep very well.'

Callie put her briefcase down and walked across the path to stand beside her.

'Neither did Braden. It's going to be a tough day for you both. I wish I could help, but I know it's better to let you do it together.'

Sophie blinked, unsure of what Callie meant and then she remembered. Today was the first day she and Braden were cleaning out Julia's stuff.

'Yes, it will be,' Sophie said softly, feeling bad that she'd forgotten. She'd been so absorbed in her own worries through the night that she hadn't given today a thought.

Callie's eyes filled with tears as she reached out and squeezed Sophie's hand. 'Look after him, Soph. He's a bit strung out this morning.'

'I will. Thanks, Callie, we'll be fine.'

'Don't worry about cooking tonight either. I'll bring Chinese home. I'll get enough for Amelia too. I think she's moving into the donga today.'

'Thanks. Now hurry up or you'll be late. Watch out for roos.'

She watched as Callie hurried to the shed and soon the throaty roar of Braden's twin cab broke the still of the morning. A few minutes later, all she could see was the dust hanging over the road east.

The kitchen was empty so Sophie grabbed a quick coffee and then went looking for Braden. It took a while but finally she found him at the back of the breezeway making up cardboard boxes and putting them onto a trailer.

'Right to start?' she said briskly.

He looked up at her and nodded. 'You look like shit.'

'Thanks, my darling brother. I'm tired.'

'Do you want to leave it until tomorrow?'

'No, come on, we'll get started. Where did you get the boxes?'

'Kent had them in the shed with the trailer. Apparently his Mum had them ready for when she packs up in a few months. We'll empty them when we're done and I'll take them back with the trailer.'

'So he got home safely?'

'Yes. He looked like shit too.'

Sophie shrugged and didn't comment as she followed Braden around the side of the yard. She didn't want to think about Kent Mason, and she sure didn't want to talk about him.

'I went to the police station yesterday and filed a report,' she said.

Braden held the door open for her as they reached the side of the house. 'I'm pleased. A bit of closure for you too, then. Maybe you won't look so miserable all the time. We've been worried about you.'

Sophie pulled a face at him. 'I shouldn't have come back to Augathella. It would have been better to start somewhere new.'

'And where would you have gone? You don't know anywhere else.'

'I can learn. I'm thinking about moving to Brisbane and taking up a traineeship if I can get one.'

'Are you sure? We'd miss you.'

'I need to get away, Bray. Especially now.'

'Why especially now?'

'Because Ros Evan's back in town.'

Braden frowned. 'And that means Jock is too?'

'Not that I know of.'

'So what's Ros got to do with your decision?'

Sophie swallowed and lifted her head to meet her brother's concerned eyes.

'She just does. I don't want to talk about it. But I saw something yesterday that really helped me make the decision. I have to escape this place. I'll never have peace if I stay. You don't want to see me moping around for the rest of my life.'

'I just want you to be happy, little sis. You gave up those two years to look after the boys, and then that jerk let you down.'

Sophie put on a brilliant smile. 'It's a new me from today. I'm sick of being unhappy. We've had some tough years, so let's go get started because I have a call to make to a Brisbane restaurant.'

'That reminds me, Callie said she'd bring Chinese home,' Braden said as they entered the side of the house where Sophie had set up her room.

'Yeah, I saw her before they left.' This time Sophie's smile was genuine. 'So did you meet Amelia?'

'I did. Bloody hell, she can talk.'

'And what about Chilli?'

'Yes, I met Chilli too. I was expecting a working dog, but he's okay. I said he can stay. Would you believe she carried her own fence in the back of her Landcruiser?'

'She is unique. I'm looking forward to getting to know her a bit more.' Sophie put her hands on her hips. 'Okay, so where do we start?'

Chapter 24

Sophie

Thursday afternoon

Many tears had been shed, but Braden and Sophie had also smiled and laughed as they cleaned out the side of the house that had been locked up for two years. Precious mementoes and Julia's jewellery had been stored safely, and now Braden sat on the sofa in the family room as Sophie vacuumed the last room.

She turned the vacuum off, left it on the rug in front of them and flopped down beside him.

'A good job done,' she said, leaning her head back on the sofa. 'And about time.'

'Thanks, Soph. That was tough, but I feel better now it's over. You know, a few weeks ago I was even thinking about asking Jon and Fallon if they'd like to swap houses.'

'What? And move the kids and Callie to the old house?'

'Yeah, it was only a thought, but I was so stressed about going through Julia's stuff, I considered it for a while. Anyway, they wouldn't have moved. I was talking to Fallon at the billy cart day and she said they love it out there.'

'I was too. She looks well.'

'Strange how things work out. Callie arriving, and then Fallon not long after.'

'Good to see some new people in the district.

'It is. Anyway, thanks again. I couldn't have done this without you.'

'It's all done now. Another step forward.'

'And what about you? You look a bit more settled now,' he said.

Sophie shrugged. 'I had something to focus on for the past two days.'

'I'll keep you busy down at the cookhouse. You can focus for as long as you like. You know, you could always stay as the permanent cook.'

'I might have to. I'm going to try to call Damon Dean before I make up my mind though.'

'You gave that traineeship up to look after the boys, didn't you?'

'It was the right thing to do at the time.'

'And I'll appreciate it for the rest of my life.' Braden grinned at her. 'They all love their Aunty Soph.'

She nudged him. 'And they love Callie too.'

'I think we'll be fine. Depends on whether Callie says yes or not.'

'Don't rush her.'

'I know. Now that we've cleared out all this, I'm ready. I'm impatient.'

'I know that well. Just bide your time. You'll know when it's right.'

Braden held her gaze. 'What about you, sis? How can I make sure you're happy?'

'I'll be fine. I'll stay out here at the station for a while and avoid town. I can order online and get the store to deliver bulk orders.'

'Why do you need to do that? Are you scared you'll see Jock?'

'No. It was seeing his sister that brought me undone. I'd prefer not to see her again.'

Braden frowned. 'Why? Because of Jock?'

She shook her head slowly. She lifted her eyes to meet her brother's. They'd grown closer again as they'd worked together over the past two days. Braden deserved to know the truth. Maybe sharing it would take a load off her.

'It's all a mess. I was a mess. I had the boys to look after and I was worried about you. But most of all, it was because of Kent.'

'Kent?' His frown deepened. 'What's she got to do with Kent?'

'Kent cheated on me with Ros Evans when we were still together. And if my gut feeling is right, he's the father of her toddler.'

'What!' Braden jumped up so quickly that the vacuum cleaner went flying.

Chapter 25

Kent

Thursday evening

Kent had suffered injuries before, but he'd never been in a situation where he only had one functioning arm. He'd always taken his health and fitness for granted, and hadn't been this incapacitated before. Sure, he'd had scrapes and bruises when he'd been a kid and he'd had a sore butt many times from rodeo falls, but he'd never known how hard it would be trying to do everything with one arm.

'Bloody hell,' he muttered on Thursday afternoon as he tried to fill the jug one-handed. He'd been updating his spreadsheet—at least his right hand was working—bringing the accounts and cattle weights up to date. Now, a man couldn't even make himself a simple cup of coffee. As Kent turned the tap off in disgust a car pulled up outside the front of the homestead and he crossed to the door.

His mood improved instantly when Braden got out of his twin cab, a six-pack of beer under his arm.

Kent used his good arm to push the screen door open and went out to the verandah.

'You're a lifesaver, mate!'

'How are you feeling?' Braden didn't look at him as he put the six-pack on the small table that sat beside the two easy chairs.

Kent manoeuvred himself carefully into the chair closest to the door. 'I'm going stir crazy. Stuck in the house. I'm finding the simplest things hard to do with one arm. Can't make a cuppa, can't cook a damn meal. I even considered inviting Jennifer out for the company.'

'Did you?'

'No, I thought better of it.' He looked curiously at Braden; he didn't seem himself tonight.

Braden pulled the top off one stubby and passed it over to him.

'Thanks, mate.' Kent leaned back in the chair and looked out to the west.

The sun was a brilliant ball of gold sitting above the horizon and the late afternoon sky was shot with shards of silver and pink. Kent's prime bull was silhouetted in the light and for the hundredth time today, Kent wished he could get outside and work. The chores were piling up; he was going to have to get help.

They sat there in silence as they drank their beers until Braden broke the silence.

'I called Jon this afternoon. He said he can give you three days a week.'

'Are you sure you can spare him?'

'I can.' Braden turned away and stared at the boundary fence.

'Are you okay, mate? Seems like something is bothering you? I can make other arrangements.'

'Sophie and I have been cleaning out the other side of the house the last couple of days.'

Kent nodded. 'That would have been hard. I can understand why you're a bit low.'

'No, I'm not low. You see, the thing is, Sophie and I had a heart-to-heart this afternoon, and she told me some pretty hard stuff.'

'About that bastard who conned her?'

Braden turned to him and his eyes were cold. 'Some of it, but most of it was about you, Kent.'

Kent put his beer down on the table and sat straight. 'About me?'

'Yeah, mate. I want you to be totally truthful with me. My sister's been pretty badly hurt and I'm looking out for her. I won't have anyone else hurt her. Her mental health is so fragile these days, she said she's going to hide out on the station. She saw something in town and she won't leave *Kilcoy* now. She's going to order the grocery supplies online and have it delivered, so she doesn't have to go to town.'

'Is Evans back in town?' Kent tried to clench his hand but the damn cast got in the way.

Braden's gaze was still square on his, and his mouth was tight. He put his beer down beside Kent's.

'No, but his sister is.' Braden didn't take his eyes off Kent's. He felt like he was under an inquisition.

'His sister? Why? Did she give Sophie a hard time too?'

'In a way, apparently. Maybe you'd like to tell me about it?'

Kent held Braden's gaze and frowned. 'Me?'

'Yep, you.'

'I don't even know his sister. Do I?'

'I don't know. Do you?' Braden's eyes narrowed. 'You telling me the truth, mate?'

'What the hell is going on, Braden? If I tell you I don't know his sister, I don't. What's her name and what's she got to do with me? Or Sophie?'

'For the last time, Kent. Are you being truthful with me?'

Kent picked up his beer and finished it on one deep draught. Not because he wasn't going to answer, but because he needed a minute to control his temper. He and Braden had been friends for a long time, but his mate was pissing him off big time with this inquisition.

He kept his voice controlled as he put the beer down on the table harder than he should have. 'I am being as truthful as I can. If you stop beating around the bloody bush and tell me exactly what you want to know, I can tell you. And I'll tell you once and once only. I don't lie. You tell me her name and I'll tell you if I know her.'

'Roslyn Evans.'

Kent frowned again and thought hard. 'I vaguely remember the name from school, I think.'

'And? Since then?'

'Since then I've never seen her, and I don't even remember what she looks like. Do you know her?'

'No. I think she left town after year ten. She came back to town when Jock did.'

'Okay. There's something you're not telling me. How about *you* be honest with me now? What the frig's going on, Braden? What's she done to Sophie, and where do I figure in all this?'

'Roslyn Evans has a child. A little boy about two years old, and Sophie suspects you're his father.'

Kent's mouth fell open as he stared at Braden. 'What the hell? Sophie thinks I have a kid? With this woman I don't even know?'

'Well, according to Sophie you know her very well. She finally admitted to me why she broke up with you. She said you slept with Ros Evans, and when she saw her little boy in town, she was really upset because he looks just like you. Maybe she's jumped to the wrong conclusion.'

'Sophie said what?' Kent pushed himself to his feet and stood over Braden. 'She reckons I slept with this Ros person—who trust me, I don't even know— and that's why she broke up with me? That's more than a bloody jumping to conclusion. It's a frigging outright lie.'

'That's what Sophie told me about an hour ago. And that's why I came straight over here.'

'Well, what I'm telling you now, is that's the biggest load of bullshit I've ever heard.'

'I hope so. I didn't believe it when Sophie first told me, but she said she knew she was right.'

'Well, I'd like to know how she's so damn sure of that. I hope you know me well enough to know that I am telling you the truth. I don't know this woman, and I've bloody well never slept with her. The only woman I've ever slept with is Sophie, and she bloody broke my heart when she left me for that jerk.' Kent's voice rose. His heart was pounding and his head began to thud again. He flopped back into the chair and put his good hand over his face. 'I'll kill the bastard. This has got Jock Evans written all over it. What a coincidence it's his sister making up this shit! Evans always wanted Sophie and he always was as jealous as hell of you and the station.

After we split, I heard him mouthing off at the pub one night, and I told him to zip it. He was bragging that when he married Sophie he'd get a share in your station. He said some pretty awful things about your situation, and he was saying how he hated having your boys with them. He saw Sophie and your boys as a way to get hold of your place.'

Braden ran a hand through his hair. 'She told me he pressured her. I feel so bloody guilty. If I'd been stronger when Julia died, none of this would have happened.'

'You can't blame yourself. Sophie made her choice. But at least she showed some sense and didn't marry him. If that bastard ever shows his face around Augathella again, I'll go for him. And I'm going to go and find that damn woman and threaten her with legal action if she so much as hints that she knew me. Who else thinks that of me? Even you believed it, Braden.'

'I'm sorry, mate. I'm sorry I had to ask you if it was true. Sophie's convinced it's the truth.'

'And you know what? That hurts more than anything. That she would believe that and not come and talk to me about it. I thought she knew me better than that. I thought she loved me, but it was all on my side, obviously.'

'Hang on, mate. You don't know what he and his sister cooked up. Plus, it all happened that week, that . . . the week that Julia had her accident. None of us were thinking straight at the time.'

'The bastard. I'll bloody take him on,' Kent growled.

'Let it go. He's gone now.'

'I'll fly up there.'

'You've got a broken arm mate. Talk to Sophie. I know you still care about her, don't you?'

'Do I?' Bitterness surged into Kent's chest, and he felt physically ill. 'I don't even know if I *could* care about someone who didn't trust me. Not only did she break my heart by believing that crap, but she hurt my parents too.'

Kent hadn't noticed Braden get up, but he felt a warm hand on his shoulder. Kent looked up, surprised to find his eyes were blurred from tears.

'Mate, I think you and Sophie need to talk this out. You need to find out the truth from her. How they convinced her, and how bloody Jock Evans ever conned her into moving in with him.'

Kent shook his head. 'I don't think I want to talk to her. I don't want to know the details. It's bad enough for me that she was with him for almost two years. How can I ever forget that?'

'How about you come back with me and talk to her?'

'No way. I need to do some thinking.'

'Kent—'

'Thanks for coming over.' Kent turned away. He felt like he was going to vomit.

'Mate, I—'

'Take the rest of the beer with you.' Kent stood and went inside, closing the door behind him.

Chapter 26

Sophie

'He won't be long, Sophie. Can I make you another coffee? Get you a wine?'

Sophie shook her head and paced along the verandah again. She was waiting for Braden to come home. Callie knew what was going on and she'd come out a few times to check on her. Braden had been gone almost two hours and Sophie was stressed to the max. Braden had believed her but insisted he was going to confront Kent.

Sophie had begged him not to go, but he'd taken off.

How long did it take to ask a question and come back home?

Once the boys were in bed Callie had come out with two mugs of coffee and stayed with her. As they sat waiting, Sophie poured her heart out. Callie couldn't believe what she told her.

'Oh, love, I'm so sorry. I knew you and Kent had been together once, but I had no idea anything like that had happened. I can't believe he did that. Trust me, I know how soul-destroying it is.'

'Well, he did and I guess I can accept that he cheated on me, but I can't believe he doesn't even acknowledge his own child. He's not the man I always thought he was. Not the man I loved.'

'Are you sure the little boy is his?'

'She said Kent didn't take responsibility for his actions. She looked at the little boy and said, "Doesn't want to know about you, does he?" '

'And you really think he's Kent's child? What made you so sure?'

'He's got dark hair like Kent.'

'And?'

Sophie stared at Callie. 'I guess that's all.'

'Look, love, from what Braden said, Jock isn't a good person. I know you were with him for a couple of years, but Braden has no time for him.'

Sophie put her head down and spoke quietly.

'I wasn't with him like you think.'

Callie frowned. 'But you've only been home a couple of months?'

'It didn't take me long to realise what Jock was like. This is going to sound stupid, but we were never a couple. We had a couple of dinner dates, and a drink at the pub one night. I moved in with him to teach Kent a lesson. I was stupid. I wanted to show Kent that he wasn't the only one who could find someone else. The fact that it was Ros's brother seemed to make it better revenge.'

'Oh, Sophie. It must have been such a dreadful time for you.'

Sophie stared into the darkness. There was still no sign of any headlights on the road. 'When Braden went to pieces, I told Jock I didn't have time to see him again because I was going to look after the boys. He offered that we all move into his place. And I took up his offer. We shared his house until he wanted to move away and I brought the boys back. You probably know that because that's when Braden advertised for a nanny.'

'Look. Here he comes.' Callie's voice had Sophie's head turning to the road. Headlights lit up the road as Braden's ute came over the hill.

'I'll leave you two to talk.' Callie reached for Sophie's mug and squeezed her hand before she went inside. 'It'll be okay, Sophie. Just remember we all love you.'

Braden didn't even drive across to the shed. He pulled the ute up at the bottom of the steps and jumped out.

Sophie walked slowly down the steps to meet her brother.

He reached out and took her hands. 'It's all right, Soph. Everything's going to be all right.'

'What? How can it be all right?' A wave of despair rolled over her, despite the grin on Braden's face.

'It's not true. None of it's true.'

'Did he know about the child?' Her voice was bleak.

How could it be all right?

'I said none of it's true. Kent didn't even know who she was. He didn't sleep with her. It was all a setup.'

Sophie felt the blood leave her head and Braden grabbed for her.

'Come on, we'll get you inside.'

An hour later, Sophie didn't know how she felt. She didn't know what to do. Callie was sitting beside Braden, and Sophie could see she was keeping a close eye on her.

'You have to go and see him, Soph. If you're worried about going yourself, I'll take you over in the morning.'

Sophie pushed herself up from the soft sofa. 'No. I'm going to go over there now. I owe Kent a huge apology. I should never have doubted him. Back then, or when I saw her with the kid.'

'It's late,' Braden said.

'It's only eight-thirty. If it looks like he's asleep, I'll go back over in the morning.'

Braden went to speak, but Callie interrupted him. 'Leave it up to Sophie, love. She knows what she wants to do. What she needs to do.' Callie stood and came across to the door to where Sophie was

179

standing. 'Just remember we're here for you. We always will be.' Callie looked up at Braden as she said that and a silent message passed between them.

'Okay. Be careful, there are a few roos about tonight.' Braden came over too, and put his arms around her. 'And what Callie said too.'

He dropped a kiss on the top of her head, and Sophie headed out to the ute.

She hadn't realised how much she was shaking until she tried to turn the key.

Chapter 27

Kent

Kent stood at the kitchen sink gripping the edge of the bench with his good hand for a long time after Braden left. Thoughts circled in his head, and he knew if his wrist hadn't been broken, he would have been in the air on the way to Innot Springs first thing in the morning to sort out Jock Evans.

But really, what good would that do?

The lie that had been told to Sophie had caused so much heartbreak. Maybe if it hadn't been told the week of Julia's accident, they would have sorted it and it wouldn't have been believed; there would have been time for questions. But that week had been horrendous, and Braden and Sophie had had too much else to deal with.

It was too late.

Kent leaned forward and rested his head on the counter, bracing himself with his good hand. It was hard to accept that Sophie had doubted him so easily.

After a few minutes, he stood, and tried to shake off the black feeling that was creeping into his heart. He'd survived the last two years, and this was what he'd needed to get over his love for her. He had more to worry about now than a woman who had doubted his love—Dad's dementia and looking after the station.

He had loved Sophie, but the person he had loved hadn't really been the woman he'd thought she was. Untrusting, and ready to drop him after believing one damn lie.

Kent turned the kitchen light off and walked into the living room. He'd lit the fire before Braden had turned up—luckily he'd had some kindling in the woodpile and hadn't had to fight with the axe one-handed. He put another log on the fire and half-closed the flue. It was going to be a cold night. He'd have to be up early in the morning; Jon was coming over to do some cattlework for him.

As he went to turn the living room light off and head for the shower, headlights played over the wall. Curious, Kent walked to the front door, and his heart stilled as Gladys, Sophie's yellow Camry pulled up outside the house.

For a minute he was tempted to turn the light off and ignore her. It was clear that Braden had told Sophie what he'd said, and she'd hot-footed it over here, thinking everything could be mended with a simple, 'here I am.'

Well, Sophie Cartwright could go take a flying leap. He didn't know if he'd ever forgive her for believing that about him. And he didn't particularly like the nasty person she'd turned into since she'd been living with Jock Evans. Braden had called it mental health, Kent called it downright bitchy.

Despite his anger, Kents's hands shook and his heart thumped as her light footsteps sounded on the steps and then along the verandah.

He walked slowly to the front door and as he opened it, her hand was raised about to knock.

For a moment their eyes met, and then Kent looked away.

'Sophie?' he said tersely. 'I was about to go to bed. What do you want?'

Her eyes widened at his rude greeting and a glimmer of guilt settled in him but he pushed it away.

'I need to talk to you,' she said.

'I've got an early start tomorrow.' He ignored the quivering of her bottom lip.

'Fair enough. Can I come in for just a moment? I really do need to talk to you.'

Reluctantly he opened the screen door and held it as she walked past him. Her familiar perfume washed over him, and his resolve weakened slightly. He gritted his teeth and made himself think of Jock Evans. The man who'd shared her bed for the past two years.

Kent turned and faced the woman he'd once loved.

Had. Remember *had.*

'So? What did you want to talk about that couldn't wait?' He folded his arms as best he could with a damn cast on and stared at her. 'Did you want to organise that date you won at the concert? I think it's expired.'

Sophie stood straight and bit her bottom lip, and her voice wavered.

He stared.

'I owe you an apology, Kent. Braden told me what you told him this afternoon. I want to tell you I'm sorry and that I do believe you.'

He shrugged. 'Good. Is that all?' His voice was harder than it had ever been in his life. But damn, how much had she hurt him? How much of his happiness and his life had she taken away by believing that lie?

Hurt crossed her face and he saw the instant that she pulled herself together. 'Yes, that's all. Thank you for your time.'

He crossed the room back to the door and held it open. 'If that's all . . .'

Her expression was blank. 'Yes, I guess that's all. Unless you want to talk?'

He raised an eyebrow. 'The time for talking is long gone. You made your choice, and I learned to live with it. Just because you know now that your choice was wrong, doesn't mean that everything should be rosy again. I've moved on, Sophie. I don't know what you expected or what you wanted, but there's nothing left for me.' The lie was bitter in his mouth, but the need to lash out and hurt her, as much as he'd hurt for the past two years, was impossible to ignore.

'Okay, I just wanted you to know I'm very sorry. I'll go and I'll leave you in peace.'

She walked past him but he couldn't let her have the last word. He reached out and put his hand on her arm. The feel of her soft skin beneath his rough fingers sent a shaft of unbearable memory rocketing though him.

'What did you think I'd do, Sophie? Welcome you with open arms? Forgive you for doubting me? Well, it's way too late for that. I know now you never loved me. If you had, there was no way you would have believed that shit.'

'I—'

'No, I don't want to hear anything more. We were over two years ago when you chose that path, so there's no point rehashing it now. Good night, Sophie. And goodbye.'

How the hell he managed to keep it together until she walked out and he shut the door behind her, Kent would never know. He'd gone so close to taking her into his arms and pretending that the past two years hadn't happened.

185

He still loved Sophie Cartwright and probably would for the rest of his life, but he wasn't going to risk his heart being broken again.

The sound of Gladys leaving his driveway broke his heart all over again.

Chapter 28

Sophie

All of Sophie's hopes and dreams sank like a stone as she drove towards the gate of *Lara Waters*. She shook her head from side to side and bit her lip as her throat ached. Regret sat in her chest like a stone.

No. How could she have ever doubted Kent? She had caused this whole mess.

All she wanted to do was keep driving. Leave this unhappiness behind her. Escape to somewhere where there was no deceit. No sadness. A place where she could find happiness again. Tears welled in her eyes and spilled over onto her cheeks. Kent hadn't even given her a chance to explain.

All she had seen was the glittering darkness of his eyes. The man who had once loved her, the man who had laughed with her. The man she had hoped to spend the rest of her life with, had looked at her with hate in his eyes. And she couldn't blame him.

But I loved him so much. I still do.

Sophie knew she'd never stopped loving Kent, even when she'd believed the worst of him.

Her heart ached as she gripped the steering wheel and turned for home.

Home?

Kilcoy Station, where Braden and Callie and the boys were about to make a happy future if Callie accepted her bother's proposal. And Sophie was sure she would. She could see the love she had for Braden and the boys in her every word and action.

Tears blurred Sophie's vision, and she flicked the headlights onto high beam as she approached the crossroads. The road to the left led to *Kilcoy Station*, and straight ahead led to Augathella and the highway to freedom.

A new future for me. A future where no one would know what a fool she'd been. Where no one knew how she'd been gullible, and thrown away true love.

She sighed, closed her eyes for a brief second, knowing she had to go home. In her hurry to get to Kent, she hadn't even brought her purse with her.

Opening her eyes, she approached the cross roads. Turning left towards Kilcoy Station she vowed she would leave in the morning.

Increasing her speed, Gladys juddered in the deep corrugations. Braden needed to get the road graded. Sophie hadn't even noticed them before in her hurry to get to Kent.

As the wheels hit a patch of bulldust, she slowed the car, and glanced to the right quickly as a shape shadowed the driver's window.

The car slewed as she slammed her foot on the brake pedal hard.

But too late.

A huge kangaroo bounced off her door and flew up onto the windscreen. The glass shattered and as she pumped the brakes again, it bounced off the bonnet and landed in front of the car. She wrenched the steering wheel to the left but Gladys was already heading off the road as the front left tyre followed the corrugation. She hit the ditch and the car began to roll.

Sophie screamed, let go of the steering wheel and covered her head with her arms. It was too late to do anything else.

Drip. Drip. Drip.

Liquid dripping on the side of Sophie's face woke her. Confused, she opened her eyes, not knowing where she was for a few seconds and why there was water dripping on her face. She wrinkled her nose as the pungent smell of petrol burned her nostrils, and it all came slamming back.

She'd rolled Gladys after hitting a roo. Her limbs trembled with shock and cold in the total dark. She tried to sit up, fumbling for her phone but she couldn't find it. She couldn't see outside or where Gladys had ended up, and she could only hope she wasn't in the irrigation channel. Her face was wet, and when she lifted her hand it came away covered in something sticky. She put her fingers to her mouth and knew straight away it was the metallic taste of blood. Her heartbeat picked up and she panicked, not knowing what to do, or where the blood was coming from

Take a deep breath, calm down.

She had to find her phone. She had to call Braden. Trying to stay calm, she braced herself and undid the seat belt and fell, jarring her arm on the door catch as she landed on the inside of the door. She scrabbled around feeling for her phone but had no luck. As she moved, the smell of petrol got stronger and she knew she had to get out of the car.

Her head spun as she pushed the door handle, and to her great relief, the door opened and she fell out onto hard dirt, not into water.

Her hand pressed into a sharp rock, and Sophie cried out as it sliced her skin open.

Pushing herself to her feet she backed away just in time as a flash of flame was followed by a loud explosion that filled the night air.

Gladys was on fire.

Blocking the thought of snakes in the knee-deep grass, Sophie ran from the car, getting as far away as she could. The orange glow split the night sky and the irrigation ditch lit up in front of her. She pulled herself up onto the edge.

She looked at the channel that snaked ahead into the dark, and then back at Gladys. If she followed the channel, it would take her back to Kilcoy Station. There was no point staying on the road; there'd be no traffic out here at this time of night. The road only led to their station and it ended there. It would be more direct to follow the irrigation channel. Her eyes gradually adjusted in the faint starlight. Taking a deep breath, she set off slipping and sliding in the soft red dust.

After only a hundred metres or so, her head began to spin and she knew she couldn't risk falling into the channel. Her legs throbbed and a cold feeling rose in her chest.

Sophie sank to her knees and began to cry.

Chapter 29

Kent

Kent paced the living room. His first thoughts were that Sophie had got everything she deserved He ran his hand through his hair, going over their conversation. Remorse filled him. He'd gone out to the veranda and watched Gladys until the tail lights disappeared and then he realised there was no point standing out there any longer. She wouldn't come back; he knew he'd been too harsh on Sophie.

He tried to be fair and put himself in the same position as she'd been in, imagining what he would have done if he'd thought she'd cheated on him.

He would have been angry and probably shut down for a while. He had to admit he wouldn't have gone looking for her.

Pride was a terrible thing.

A destructive emotion.

But no matter how he tried to imagine it, he knew he could never imagine the circumstances of that week when Julia died.

He'd give it a few days, and go and see Sophie.

Too wired to go to bed, he headed to the kitchen and was trying to fill the kettle when the phone rang.

He crossed to the bench, glanced at the clock and picked up the handset. 'Kent Mason.'

'Kent. I'm sorry to bother you and I know it's probably the worst timing ever, but I just wanted to check that Sophie was still with you. Just tell me to butt out, once you reassure me.'

'Sophie? No, she only stayed a short time. She left here a couple of hours ago.'

'She left?' Braden's reply came quickly.

'Yes.'

'She's not home yet. I thought you two must have made your peace when she didn't come back.'

'She left here about nine. She only stayed ten minutes.'

'What? Did she say where she was going?'

'No. Are you sure she's not home?'

'Positive. I've been waiting for her and assumed she was still at your place.'

'Would she have gone into town?

'I doubt it. Jeez, I hope she hasn't broken down.'

Or worse, Kent thought.

'I'll go and look for her. I'll follow the road to your place,' Kent said.

'Thanks, mate. I'll start this end. Hopefully one of us will come across her.'

'We should do. If she's broken down, one of us will find her. She would have had the sense to stay in the car. It's cold out there.'

'Right. I'll see you in twenty.' Braden's voice was tight.

Kent grabbed his keys and raced out to his ute. He ignored the pain in his arm as he put it into gear and dropped the clutch. The wheels spun as he accelerated down the driveway. At the gate he turned the ute onto the back road that led to Charleville. The road was dry and there had been no wind. His headlights lit up the fresh tracks of Gladys's tyres in the soft red dirt. He kept his eyes dead ahead as he sped along the dirt road in the dark.

The lefthand turn off to Kilcoy Station wasn't far ahead. As he approached the intersection, he looked for her tyre tracks and relief filled him as they veered to the left. Kent swung the wheel to the left and stayed in top gear to save his arm. Ahead there was a faint glow above the road and his eyes narrowed.

Panic clenched his chest as he realised it was fire.

'Jesus, no!' he yelled as he accelerated down the corrugated road and then swerved to the side of the road before the fire ahead. Almost falling out of the vehicle, Kent found his balance and ran across to the still smoking wreck. In the middle of the road was the carcass of a huge roo, and he could see what had happened. Sophie had hit the roo, and the car had rolled onto the passenger side.

Frantic, he put his hand to his eyes and looked into the darkness, but there was no sign of Sophie. Panic closed his throat as he considered the worst. He knew he was responsible for this.

He'd refused to listen to the woman he still loved and he'd sent her out into the night.

The rumble of a vehicle came from ahead and in the distance, he saw the lights of Braden's twin cab approaching from *Kilcoy Station*. He took another step towards the smouldering vehicle, his whole body tense, praying she had got out.

As he walked around it, his spirits lifted as he noticed the dirt beside the car was disturbed. Relief filled him as he saw footsteps leading into the bush.

Thank God. She'd managed to get out; Braden must have picked her up and was coming to tell him she was okay.

Kent sat on the side of the road, his body still shaking from seeing her car burned out. He waited for Braden to reach him. A couple of minutes passed and he managed to get his breath back; the tension easing a little.

The instant he saw Sophie he would tell her how he felt. The thought of how close he had gone to losing her steeled his resolve. He stood as Braden's twin cab approached.

Kent's spirits plummeted when he saw that Braden was alone. Braden's twin cab slewed to a stop, and he jumped out, his face white.

'Holy hell. Is that Sophie's Camry?'

'Yes, it's Gladys, but look.' Kent grabbed his arm. 'It's all right, mate. She got out. Look here, you can see her footsteps. I thought you must have picked her up down the road.'

'No, I didn't see her and I was looking. Jesus, Kent, she must be hurt. She could be anywhere out there.' Braden hurried across to Sophie's Gladys. 'Fucking roos. She's hit a fucking roo and rolled.'

'Calm down, mate. We'll find her. You take my ute and go bush on the other side of the road. Put the headlights on high beam It's higher than yours. I'll go on foot on this side and see if I can see any tracks in the dirt.' Kent ran back and grabbed a flashlight from his ute, closely followed by Braden.

Braden jumped into Kent's ute and headed into the scrub on the other side of the road. Kent walked past the wreck lighting the way with the strong flashlight, keeping his eyes on footsteps in the red dirt. He called out when he spotted where she'd left the road.

'Sophie,' he yelled. 'Sophie, can you hear me?'

The only sound was the faint hum of his ute as Braden ploughed through the low bush on the other side. Ahead was an irrigation channel, half-full with brown water. He reached the edge and shone the light ahead, and sure enough her footsteps were along the edge.

'Good girl,' he muttered. Sophie would have known it was quicker to follow the channel home. He hurried back to the road and jumped into Braden's ute and drove back the way he'd walked.

There was still no sign of her. Every hundred metres or so, he leaned out the window and checked that he could still see her footsteps in the fine red dirt.

The last time he slowed to check, her footsteps had disappeared. Kent stopped the car and climbed out and ran back along the channel. About fifty metres back, the track stopped. He held his hand to his eyes and scanned the bush around him.

'Sophie, where are you?'

About a hundred metres towards the road, there was a stand of gidgee scrub silhouetted by the moonlight. Kent paused as a faint cry came from that direction.

A bird? Or a cry for help.

'Sophie,' he yelled again, flashing his light ahead as he ran towards the stand of low trees.

'Braden?'

He stumbled as her voice came from that direction.

'Sophie, where are you?'

As he got closer, there was a movement to his left and as he turned the light, Sophie pushed herself to her feet. 'Kent?'

He covered the distance quickly and took her in his arms, his eyes scanning her for injuries.

'Sophie, my love. Are you all right? Are you hurt?'

'What did you call me?'

'I'm so sorry. It was all my fault. I should never have spoken to you like that.'

She looked up at him. 'What did you call me, Kent?'

'What I should have told you before, instead of being a prize bastard. I love you, Sophie. I always have and I always will. I died a hundred deaths when I saw Gladys burning. I thought you were still inside her.'

Kent closed his eyes as Sophie's arms crept around his waist, and he barely noticed the throbbing of his wrist. He lowered his head and rested his cheek against hers. 'I'm never going to let you go again, Soph. I love you. Can you forgive me for the way I spoke to you?'

Her eyes were wide as she pulled back and stared at him. 'It was all my fault.

'No, it was mine. Are you hurt?'

'Just a bit of a sore head, and I cut my hand on a rock. I'm all right. Do you really mean what you said?'

'Of course I do. I've never stopped loving you.'

'And I love you, Kent. I always have. I'm so sorry.' Her voice was thick with tears.

'We've got a lot of talking to do, Soph, but first we need to let Braden know you're okay. If it wasn't for this blasted arm, I'd carry you to the ute.'

He put his good arm around her and kept his eyes on hers until they reached the twin cab. Her cheeks were flushed and she was smiling.

'Whatever happens, whatever we have to talk about, it's okay,' he said.

'Kent, I need you to know one thing right now.' Sophie put her hands on his shoulders. 'I never slept with Jock. It was just a share arrangement to start with and he was helping me out. I need you to know that right now. We can talk later.'

Joy burst through Kent as he held her close again. 'We can talk later. We have all the time in the world.'

Sophie lifted her arms around his neck and pulled Kent's head closer to hers.

'Kiss me?' She pressed her lips against his mouth. 'Please, kiss me, Kent. It's been such a long time.'

An unbelievable feeling ran through him as she closed her eyes and his lips claimed hers.

Sophie opened her eyes as he murmured against her lips. 'Way too long.'

Kent was still kissing Sophie when Braden drove up a few minutes later.

Epilogue

Two days later

Sophie stood beside Kent in the living room of *Lara Waters* when he called his parents. According to the itinerary on the fridge, their ship was docking in Brisbane this morning.

'Mum. Hi, it's me.' His arm was around her. 'I've got someone who'd like to say hello to you. And I have some news I know you'll be very excited about.'

Kent handed the phone to Sophie but kept his arm around her. She leaned into him, unable to believe the happiness of the past two days. She kept pinching herself, waiting to wake up, but it was true.

She and Kent were back together. And. . .

'Hello, Rhonda,' she said shyly. 'It's Sophie.'

'Sophie? How lovely. It sounds like my son actually listened to me for a change. How are you, sweetie? It's so lovely to hear your voice again.'

'I'm really good,' Sophie replied with a smile up at Kent. 'Really good. I'd love to see you. We were wondering what your plans were as we'd like you to . . . hang on, I'll put Kent back on. I want him to tell you the news.'

Sophie leaned into Kent as he took the phone from her.

'I know you were going to stay in Brisbane for a while, but we just wanted to know when you'll be home.'

Kent smiled at Sophie as his mother obviously wanted to know more.

'Well, we want to know because we want to set the date for our engagement party.'

Sophie grinned up at him as she heard Rhonda's delighted squeal through the phone.

'Next week? You're going to rush home, Mum? Yes, we'll be here. Sophie and I aren't going anywhere, are we?'

'No, we're not,' she said as she reached up to kiss her fiancé.

##

Later that afternoon, Sophie parked Kent's ute near the shed at *Kilcoy Station*. Braden had asked them to come over and babysit the boys. Since the night Kent had found her near the irrigation channel, they hadn't been apart. Sophie stayed at *Lara Waters,* and there had been many hours spent talking.

Kent swung his good arm around her shoulders as they walked to the house. It sounded like there was a battle going on inside, and sure enough Petie came racing out, closely followed by Nigel.

'Aunty Soph,' Nigel said urgently. 'Don't tell Rory where we're hiding.'

Two of the boys' dogs followed them into the dog kennels, and then all was quiet.

'You ready for a fun night?' Sophie asked Kent with a teasing grin.

'Will a broken wrist get me out of playing hide and seek?'

'Not a chance.'

Callie came out of the kitchen and hugged them both. 'Fabulous news, you pair. I'm so happy for you. Braden couldn't wait to get home and tell me the other night. The best news ever!'

'Where are you pair off to tonight?' Kent asked. 'Is there something on in Augathella?'

Callie shrugged. 'I have no idea. Braden said it's a surprise and told me to get dressed up.'

Sophie hid her smile. She knew exactly what her brother had planned for tonight. If all went to plan, the engagement party in two weeks would be a double celebration. She hadn't told Kent what was going on, but he'd soon know.

They waved a nervous-looking Braden and a bemused Callie off, just before Kent was roped into the game of hide and seek.

Sophie stood on her tiptoes and kissed him before he headed off with the three boys. 'I'll go and get some dinner sorted. Do you mind if I ask Amelia to come over? I feel a bit guilty that I haven't been here to cook. The whole crowd of contractors arrive tomorrow, so I'm going to have to start work for Braden.'

'As long as you come home to me every night.' Kent kissed her and the three boys made gagging noises.

'Not you too,' Rory exclaimed with disgust. 'Dad and Callie are always kissy-kissy too.'

'Love is grand,' Kent said with a laugh. 'You'll find out one day.'

'Rory's already got a girlfriend at school,' Nigel teased.

'I have not!'

'You have so!'

'Have fun.' Sophie threw Kent a smile as she headed up to the dongas to see Amelia.

As she walked to the accommodation area, an unfamiliar ute came along the road from the back of the property. She waited and was surprised to see Kent's singing partner, Ben Riley in the cab.

'Hey, Ben. Are you after Braden? He's not home.'

'No. I knew he was going out. I just have to check on the foundations of the new donga he's building. He asked me to check the concrete thickness. I had to come out and see Jon and Fallon, so I came across the back way.'

'Kent's here too,' she said looking down at the engagement ring on her left hand. They hadn't shared the news outside family yet. She'd let Kent tell his friend after they told Jacinta.

'Great, haven't seen him since the rodeo. I'll catch him on my way out. This won't take long. Is that the dongas over there?'

'Yes, there's only one of the two occupied at the moment. The new one's pegged out at the far end.'

'Thanks. I won't be long.'

Sophie detoured via the cookhouse. She'd placed an order online at Kent's place yesterday and Callie had asked them to deliver it to the cool room in the cookhouse.

All was well, and she closed the cookhouse door behind her, planning the meal to feed the group tomorrow night.

'It's a bloody danger!' Her head flew up as Ben's angry voice reached her as she approached the dongas. 'It needs to be in a kennel or in a muzzle.'

'Well, if you spoke to *him*—not *it*—properly and not just barged past, he—'

Sophie didn't hear the rest of what Amelia had to say because Ben's roar drowned out her words.

'So it's my fault your bloody dog bit me?'

'Oh no,' Sophie muttered under her breath as she hurried over.

Ben and Amelia stood glaring at each other, her hand at the scruff of her dog's neck. If dogs could glare, Chilli was glaring at Ben too.

'Hi Amelia,' Sophie said brightly, ignoring the tension filling the air. 'I just came down to ask you to the house for dinner tonight, but it looks like you guys need to chill out a bit. How about you both come with me now, and we can have a beer or a wine? Ben, you've knocked off now, haven't you?'

He nodded. 'I have.'

'Well, both of you come up to the house and I'll tell Kent you're on the way. I think he'll be pleased to have a break from the boys.'

Sophie turned and headed back to the house to tell Kent they had company.

It would be an interesting way to spend the time, while she waited for Braden and Callie to come back.

Hopefully engaged.

Sophie smiled as she lifted her hand and her engagement ring sparkled in the late afternoon sunlight.

UNTIL THE NEXT STORY...

Will Braden and Callie tie the knot?
When is Fallon's baby going to arrive?
Will Sophie work at Kilcoy Station?

The girls' stories continue in *Outback Winds* as we learn more about those who live in the district.

Amelia Foley has always lived on the land. Sent to the best boarding schools, her parents hoped for a professional career in the city for their only daughter. Five strapping sons can run the family station according to her father. But Amelia hates city life and sets off to work as a jillaroo on Kilcoy Station.

Local shire building inspector, Ben Riley, visits Kilcoy Station to advise Braden Cartwright on the new buildings he is planning as the station expands. After a run-in with Amelia's sidekick—Chilli, the golden retriever—Ben insists Amelia comes to town to attend the local dog obedience classes.

As the jillaroo and the inspector spend more time together, attraction grows quickly.

But Ben can't wait to do his time in the bush and move to the city; Amelia wants to make a success of her career on the huge cattle spread.

Will his growing feelings for Amelia be enough for Ben to stay in the bush? And will she give her heart to a man who wants to leave all that she loves?

The Augathella Girls series.

Book 1: Outback Roads -The Nanny

Book 2: Outback Sky -The Pilot

Book 3: Outback Escape – The Sister

Book 4: Outback Winds – The Jillaroo

Book 5: Outback Dawn – The Visitor

Book 6: Outback Moonlight – The Rogue

Book 7: Outback Dust – The Drifter

Book 8: Outback Hope – The Farmer

If you would like to stay up to date with Annie's releases, subscribe to her newsletter here:

http://www.annieseaton.net

OTHER BOOKS from ANNIE

Whitsunday Dawn
Undara
Osprey Reef
East of Alice (November 2022)

Porter Sisters Series
Kakadu Sunset
Daintree
Diamond Sky
Hidden Valley
Larapinta

Pentecost Island Series
Pippa
Eliza
Nell
Tamsin
Evie
Cherry
Odessa
Sienna
Tess
Also available in three boxed sets
Books 1-3
Books 4-6
Books 7-10.

The Augathella Girls Series
Outback Roads
Outback Sky
Outback Escape
Outback Wind
Outback Dawn
... plus more to come

Sunshine Coast Series
Waiting for Ana
The Trouble with Jack
Healing His Heart
Sunshine Coast Boxed Set

The Richards Brothers Series
The Trouble with Paradise
Marry in Haste
Outback Sunrise
Richards Brothers Boxed Set

Bondi Beach Love Series
Beach House
Beach Music
Beach Walk
Beach Dreams
The House on the Hill

Second Chance Bay Series
Her Outback Playboy
Her Outback Protector
Her Outback Haven
Her Outback Paradise

OUTBACK ESCAPE

The McDougalls of Second Chance Bay-Boxed Set

Love Across Time Series
Come Back to Me
Follow Me
Finding Home
The Threads that Bind
Love Across Time Boxed Set

Bindarra Creek
Worth the Wait
Full Circle
Secrets of River Cottage (Nov 22)

Four Seasons Short and Sweet
Ten Days in Paradise
Follow the Sun

Others
Deadly Secrets
Adventures in Time
Silver Valley Witch
The Emerald Necklace
Christmas with the Boss
Her Christmas Star
An Aussie Christmas Duo (the two Christmas novellas)

About the Author

Annie lives in Australia, on the beautiful north coast of New South Wales. She sits in her writing chair and looks out over the tranquil Pacific Ocean.

She writes contemporary romance and loves telling stories that always have a happily ever after. She lives with her very own hero of many years and they share their home with Toby, the naughtiest dog in the universe, and Barney, the ragdoll puss, who hides when the four grandchildren come to visit.

Stay up to date with her latest releases at her website: **http://www.annieseaton.net**